I0594294

# AFGHAN
## Song of the Desert

N.B.J.Clayton

Copyright © N.B.J.Clayton, 2020

N.B.J.Clayton asserts the moral right to be identified as the owner of this work.

All rights reserved. No part of this publication may be reproduced, stored in a retrieval system, or transmitted in any form, by any means: electronic, mechanical, photocopying, recording or otherwise, without the prior permission of the copyright owner of this book.

This book is sold subject to the conditions that it shall not be resold, hired out or otherwise circulated, except in its original binding.

Publication data:

Afghan - Song of the Desert, 1st ed.
ISBN: 978-0-6487672-5-1

DRA012000   Drama/Australian & Oceanian
FIC014000   Fiction/Historical/General
POE010000   Poetry/Australian & Oceanian

Epic Poems by This Author:

Kibeho: An Epic Poem
Orcinus Orca: Song of the Ocean
Hollandia Nova, 1712: Song of the Coast

## SETTING THE SCENE

A little town of Australia's past,
Adheres to new name for the people vast,
What was once called Hergott Springs,
Is now Marree where desert wind sings.

The year is 1883 to be sure,
On this day, 20th Dec no more,
What was a groomed settlement small,
Is now a town and standing tall.

Its growth more rapid than any previous year,
It started as a camp for workers most dear,
An overland telegraph line of sturdiness to build,
Across the great expanse, the responsibility of this guild.

Ethnic population growing, flowing water beneath barge,
Fewer white than blacks, seemingly true and at large,
A nickname employed to accompany its growth,
Christened Little Asia by many, though many do loathe.

Here they arrive, having come to roost,
Afghans and their camels to population boost,
To call this home more than sixty families firmly stand,
This place for Afghans amidst Australian sand.

# AFGHAN

An Afghan works for near pittance, a smear,
A quarter that the salary of the white man so near,
So no stranger should it be, great advantage took,
Their service taken for granted, at first glance, at first look.

The white mans' bullocks are no match at all,
No match for the camels which seem never to stall,
A single humped dromedary of great worth,
Here for the haul they bring Afghan great mirth.

An Afghan is not just from Afghanistan,
A darkish and very ethnic man,
An Australia is from white background,
Convict, immigrant, or from around.

These Afghans come to work as any other,
To soil and desert sands, there are none tougher,
From Kashmir, Punjab, Persia, most sturdy,
Great men from Egypt and even from Turkey.

Easy it is to grow business here,
Where camels cost little to rear,
For they are to become part of the bush, of the desert around,
Ships of the desert, of sand, and every mound.

Cost effective and sturdy, heavenly great,
They do their work, pull their own weight,
More than a bullock team, for which Afghan hate,
Amongst farmers and homesteaders, are favoured first rate.

Little to no water and no shodding needed,
Little maintenance required and easily tended,
Bullock teams need the more expensive hay,
And less hardy they are that most farmers say nay.

Horse teams too appear to fare little better,
Appearing as though shackled, strangled by fetter,
Taking from white purse most expense,
To employ them goes against good common sense.

New lease to life was government reaction,
To get the railroad built in good fashion,
From Marree to north as fast as they may,
No room for idleness, no room to stray.

Marree was now the centre of attention,
Attracting much work and camels the mention,
Farmers from all over need to get goods to port,
Needing to rent reliable service and good sport.

Supplies are needed by them, their ration,
And someone to get goods from farm to station,
No better way than to bargain, service as cheap as one agrees,
To get the move on the nation, be busy as bees.

Settlements, homesteads and farmers, they stack,
Of Birdsville, Strzelecki and Oodnadatta track,
And less trodden trails to outposts and more,
All around this vast area, transport from farmer, to store.

# AFGHAN

Alice springs and Broken Hill,
Coolgardie and Innamincka still,
For hundreds of miles around the trend,
Trend for transportation, there is no end.

Area prone to floods and drought,
Sandstorms an upheaval sound out,
Colonists desire good time, this you must maintain,
Get their merchandise to consumers on time by train.

And in Marree a police station, much smaller than any other,
With three men of uniform tending their flock, don't smother,
A general store and post office can be easily seen,
And a few others as well, though little more between,

For all the more it is a place like depository,
A place to deliver goods and collect amidst story,
A place to conduct business, to converse, and never be late,
Rely on the railroad and tell old stories to mate.

The cemetery is as racist as the rest of town,
Split into three quarters to all is renown,
Aboriginal, Afghan and white,
Even here in growth there is great spite.

Derived from an old aboriginal word, Marree was born,
Bore from 'many possums', a story, possums a thorn,
The possums now replaced by camels of varied colour,
They too are everywhere you care to look amidst splendour.

Now in the year 1884, more than 1500 camels here,
Single hump variety, a mosque, date palms near,
A place of worship amidst this date palm lair,
System of flowing water for ablution before prayer.

Small comforts in the bush, desert plains wide,
Flies and ants galore here do thrive and abide,
Forty or fifty degrees does harbour respect,
Hell on earth though people do not neglect.

Hot during the day is unspeakable truth,
And cold by night you chatter until sore tooth,
A desert as many other in seamless drought,
A place to scorn, a horrid place to live, no doubt.

But they come all the same,
Be it many men or a few dame,
Do their work and try to live,
Such is life, and for some life do give.

And so Christmas of 1883 has well and truly concluded,
No Christmas cheer about, population deluded,
But telegraph poles are growing, trees uprooted,
From August 1870 to July 1872 has been noted.

And to Stretch across bare land and flooded plains,
From Port Augusta to Darwin, build a rail for trains,
A time of legendary engineering and great skill,
Cultures do not mix, though only a few wish to kill.

# AFGHAN

So don't forget the date of this song,
This is 1884, do not get it wrong,
Other dates may appear to be of mention,
But 1884 is most important, no need to question.

## THE ARRIVAL

Nak Kadir is 42, a little long in the teeth,
Gums well parted to reveal stains beneath,
Well stained beyond his year,
But nowhere near as some do appear.

But he wore no smile, at this minute, today,
For a scar across mouth and lips, pessimistic and grey,
Lips held back by restraint from forming such in his despair,
Tissue forever damaged beyond repair.

But affect his speech it did not, no, that was absurd,
For this was a man much accustomed to word,
A friendly man with damaged background,
He has come here for a penny to be earnt, not found.

Standing years before at the gateway of Marree,
He had come to stay, regardless of what may be,
To find his fortune through hard work not wrong,
To call Australia his new home amongst the growing throng.

Steeped in desire to earn extended families respect,
Family residing in Afghanistan, he has no regret,
He does all he can to merit good word, no liar,
And keep at bay a majority of sinful ways and desire.

# AFGHAN

He is awaiting his new worker to call,
A man named Abdul Hassan, apparently handsome and tall,
A 23 year old, no devil, a picture formed in mind,
Whom had a wife and two young, who had been left behind.

Nak surveyed the iron line, from station and down,
Seemingly touched by the best commodity in town,
Turban upon his head, dirty at best,
And a robe of nation cast, for working, not rest.

He had been patient all day for the train,
Its arrival delayed, for no good reason, but a pain and a stain,
No message of lateness was received upon wire so grey,
Telegraph line drooping silently before cooling of day.

Muslim men were quite exotic to the eye,
Though hatred for the most you cannot deny,
From Marree, far north and south abide,
Hard to find one without camel at his side.

Immigration was thick in the 1860s and more,
With their camels to accompany men and their store,
A mix of man and beast, an oiled machine to beat,
Well suited to Australia and the desert heat.

Only 18 men had arrived in 1838, 22 years before,
Growth of importation staggering, seemingly passed by law,
Importation of camels to grow, some saying exponentially,
Quite a phenomenon to see, really quite expectantly.

They were a required asset to this new country,
A new home to take to breast: ethnically contrary,
European men despising camels with grimace,
No love they held for the single humped menace.

But Afghan men loved these beasts, never to neglect,
Treated them fair and gained much, much respect,
Together they were a team, to work hard all day: so it would seem,
Afghans love their camels, eyes never lie, they gleam.

It's a loathing feeling that all white men hold,
Spitting in the wake of all they have, be told,
Not jealous at all, just racist and unfair,
Racist and rude, stubbornly confirmed by fatal stare.

Even after so long at work, working hard as all men should,
Afghan men were without doubt, clearly misunderstood,
White men gave no proof, no time to clarify,
Why they hated them to the core, from ground to sky.

Birdsville was once known as Diamantina Crossing,
Many small homesteads here, and slightly engrossing,
Lake Harry Homestead is one of many, upon desert land,
Mulka Homestead, another to mention, neither that grand.

Birdsville, to town of Marree, was like good brother,
Pastoral properties around, so vast as to smother,
Each the centre of its own action amidst barren landscape shout,
Like core of gold and wealth with veins stretching out and about.

# AFGHAN

Afghans were here to earn money and send it home,
White man to carve fortune, pastoral lands, forming a tome,
Each endeavour in their own way, to gain their need,
Both striving hard to achieve their ultimate greed.

It was then that Nak heard something warming and familiar,
In the distance a train approaching, sound of bliss to his ear,
Abdul Hassan would be here soon, to aid with camels: a tool,
At Nak's heal, to stand and to work, as was desired and the rule.

Nak then briefly thought of his dear friend,
Shir Adji an accomplice to unwritten contract's end,
His partner to gift hard work, he wished to uphold his name,
He was 33yrs old and ugly as sin, so ugly to eye it was a shame.

A few coins giggled in Nak's pocket, hence not spent, refrained,
Reminding him of Shir and the job most recently obtained,
A homesteader, come farmer, needed Abdul and his camel string,
To deliver goods, commencing tomorrow, vast supplies to bring.

From Marree to just south of Birdsville they would have to tend,
A good long trip to near Pandie Pandie, to test Abdul to no end,
Two jobs here knitted into one,
Much money to be had if working finger to the bone,

Birdsville was fitted with three stores and chemist, parts, a lith,
Butchers shop, two hotels, and one lonely blacksmith,
Though blacksmith, no need the cameleers required of him,
For camels need not be shodded, and no hoof requiring trim.

This homestead near Pandie Pandie also required wool delivered,
Taken from their homestead to Marree, a town tethered,
To be deposited by train, to Port Augusta please,
Then to Adelaide and shops with much glee to appease.

Large responsibility for all through the year, and more to explore,
Three men tasked with many jobs, vastly different, galore,
Their camels worth their weight in gold at time of portage,
Men and their pets working as one, of conviction no shortage.

Rely Nak does on Abdul being a good man true, maturity grown,
As Shir was reliable with his eyes reflecting their tint of brown,
Shir, a good man, was to be married this very night,
To Aboriginal lady, she would treat him right.

Each three needed the other,
Reliance on each as though their mother,
Commanding over many camels does require few men,
But each must be worthy, each one worth ten.

Importance of work could never be underestimated,
Any job could ruin them if not planned, or purposely machinated,
They need to compete, far and wide, against other cameleers,
The name Faiz Mahomet, for one, comes to many ears.

Faiz is a learned man of strength,
A forwarding agent of many years length,
A general carrier of goods in great number,
He is profitable, always alert, never at slumber.

# AFGHAN

Faiz was a *jemadar*, had been for many a year,
More than four hundred employed and working full gear,
Mainly at Karachi Wharves he displayed his strength, did flourish,
Well respected by all and to all below he seemingly did nourish.

Nak pondered the life to fall Abdul,
Not yet arrived but work ready and available,
He in the Ghantown of small town spoke,
Where homes were built so cheaply as to make a joke.

The road parallel was extremely busy and of great credit,
Its hardened surface portraying wide use and to all a benefit,
Countless hooves having trodden this way in the past,
Many more millions to follow in future, forever to last.

Another camel string and Afghans was passing by,
Considering it Faiz Mohamed's would not be a lie,
One cameleer to every ten camels did steer,
Nak himself desired eight to control and to treat as though peer.

Yes, there was much work in handling a camel,
Work in rearing them too, prior to extensive travel,
Not to mention the young they bore unto the world scene,
Born into the lap of work, it waiting; dirty, never clean.

He brushed once more the flies from his face,
The air stifling and stinking and hot, no display of grace,
His skin hardened by the unrelenting heat,
The rays of the sun seemingly cooking him as though meat.

## A BRIEF TOUR

The breaking of the train was methodical screeching,
The sound of which was far reaching,
Engine and moving parts screaming out loud,
Puffs of steam appear, a stream of billowing cloud.

Faces in windows peering out now,
Hard faces all to greet with enthusiasm low,
Creases and cuts in flesh adorn,
Many hours hard labour, stoutly worn,

The engine now fully stationary, much commotion both in and out,
Doors opening and men with baggage pouring out,
And then from last carriage a tall man does appear,
Afghan in semblance drawing Nak's most studying leer.

The man is handsome and with turban, it does adorn,
Pantaloon trousers truly well worn,
Trousers dark in colour but turban not,
High boots too, fine shirt, not rot.

Abdul wore a smile, happy and wide,
Nak's a grimace from past, from battle's tide,
Abdul's story a near reflection of his employer,
And Nak's a semblance of war, the destroyer.

# AFGHAN

For no real peace can be gained from conflict,
Only bad memories and scars, of joy they do restrict,
Taking sanity away for all so that they do suffer,
In silent pain and pain from much more, from other.

"Are you Abdul Hassan?" Nak does ask,
"Yes, I am he, and ready for task."
"I'm Nak Kadir, I'm sure you are aware,"
His facial grimace demands temporary stare.

"Do you have much with you?" does Nak enquire,
"I have nothing with me, no materialistic desire,
No spare clothes, no blanket for sleep,
No socks for change, or clip for money to keep."

"As poor as the poor, but keen to work hard,
No song for me to whistle, not even a bard,
My soul and good nature is all I have here
It is what I hold most, I hold it most dear."

So says Nak with a stare,
"You have nothing to bear,
Nothing at all but free of burden,
Ready to work hard in this furnace, this horrid garden."

They both shake hands and acknowledge a bond,
They are one and the same, as fish in a pond,
They both appear happy, happy and free,
Two birds of a feather and soon to be three.

"Come with me," says Nak at last,
"Come meet Shir Adji before we set to task,
He's a friend of years past,
Someone to trust to the very last."

Abdul waves a fly from upon his face,
Waving off fly in what is Aussie salute with grace,
For waving flies away from nose, face and cheek, from head,
Becoming second nature: mated: like a needle to thread.

Nak said: "The flies here will drive you crazy,
Just keep waving off, don't get lazy,
Annoying they may be,
But you get used to them, you'll see."

"It's like the work we get with colonist, plenty to be had,
Though good at job you must prove, having patience is not bad,
Once farmer is convinced and consolidated,
Your service will hence be well faired, well rated."

"More work than you can handle will fall your way,
But tough it out, remain focussed, and never stray,
Prove yourself strong and reliable to all confronted,
Be true to your word and ethics, never be routed."

Abdul said: "The office in which I applied,
Advised good work be had, he has not lied,
I care not how hard I need to work,
So long as it keeps my future from unfortunate murk."

# AFGHAN

Nak is pleased: "You must learn a new way, new rope,
Gain what you can, be reinforced by all hope,
Do not take advantage of any easy road, avoid the easy route,
Keep your head high, and grow from experience, you'll sprout."

"Stay with me, you will have nothing to regret,
I treat men well, and for one to stray I do not let,
Men like Faiz Mahomet, if you excuse me please,
Some of his workers grow lazy in attitude and tease."

"We will depart tomorrow for our first appointment,
A homesteader turning farmer near Birdsville, our agreement,
Sometimes we travel by night, when it's cool,
Especially during Ramadan, we try to follow each rule."

Nak asked further: "So from Kandahar you are?
"Yes," replied Abdul, with half guilty stare, memory afar,
"Well, I am from Kabul, and Shir from Karachi,
You shall be our good friend, and we, good companions for thee.

And Nak pondered more on the past,
To hear all the truth to the very last,
"Did you leave Afghanistan before the war,
Before the British moved in, before all the gore?"

"After," replied Nak, unsteady in breath,
"I fought against the British, to do so till death,
For two years I bore body against them,
And not long after I came to Australia seeking my gem."

Abdul then said: "Receive your gem you may or may not,
But regardless of future you are giving it your best shot,
You once fought the British in your past,
But now you basically serve them in your days so vast."

Nak stopped temporarily upon his feet,
"I serve no one, and for this I shall not be discreet,
I serve my ambition, and you my new employee,
I am as devoted to work as was against Britain, you'll see."

"I shall not be a servant to the British,
But must convey I need work to fill my dish,
Nak then added: "We are both prisoners here as you know,
Getting our lives on track for money and into purse we stow."

Abdul enjoyed good honesty, people being up front,
Nak said: "I was a tribesman back home, maintaining my wont,
But never felt like a pheasant, whether treated as such or not,
For in heart I was forever of own mind, and all good was begot"

"But now I am here, treated as I desire,
I command over my future, I am no liar,
But hard work it will surely be, I do attest,
But always I will do, for you, my very best."

And Nak continued more with solemn song,
"Forever looking over my shoulder, as though wrong,
Seeing if eyes recognise me for all I have done,
But in the end I think I have won."

# AFGHAN

"I have divided myself from previous incursion,"
Continued Nak as though it were his mission,
"There is no truly escaping their cause or true wit,
Though I shall also never truly join it."

"This country need me more than I need it,
But remain here I shall as I feel I do fit,
For without my service they would shrivel and die,
We use them more than we actually rely."

Abdul then felt to remind Nak once more,
A letter he sent to Port Augusta, an office of lore,
"I served in General Robert's Camel Corps, travelled far,
I was in the march of 1880 from Kabul to Kandahar."

"I know," replied Nak, for he had arranged this day,
Asked friend in Port Augusta to gain worker before they stray,
Abdul had arrived with shipment in 1884
Along with 259 camels in hull, the ship's store.

Nak continued: "It is true to be wise,
Never hide truth behind any disguise,
I served against the British and you served with them,
Neither of us have blossomed from this, their poisonous stem".

"My friend, Jehangir, does well I must agree,
Did his search as though he were me,
Plucked you by choice from a wroughting crowd,
Making a choice of which he can be proud."

"And I trust in his good judgement,
Of his idealisms and character assessment,
Seeing first hand the character you carry,
Understanding you as though his wife did marry."

"Yes," said Abdul, looking Nak in the eye,
"He plucked me right out of there, as plump bird from pie,
He showed me the way to fruitful life and employment,
Into your very hands, and, seemingly, for my enjoyment."

Nak reflects on the past: "Jehangir is a good man to know,"
And changes tone: "I understand him more as I grow,
But our escape was no different than what was yours,
We do all we can to stay alive, pick and choose our own chores."

"We all served those we needed to serve,
But now serve ourselves with great nerve,
I sometimes regret my actions in Afghanistan,
But I had to defend against the invasion of British man."

"But speak of it no more, I wish to advise,
War is a strange bedfellow for the wise,
And wiser we grow with work to be found,
Working our feet into the very ground."

"We are all Durannis, though different than Mahomet,
For he threatens our job prospects as each is met,
Faiz is far better than Abdul Wade,
A common and despicable Ghilzai made."

# AFGHAN

And Nak trailed off, his thoughts were poison rort,
For the Durranis were not really his sort,
Durranis formerly known as Abdulis,
Nak was just trying to provide similarities.

Abdulis and Abdul, similar in some way,
Strange comparison, not dressed in black, but grey,
But he put nought in it and thought of it no more,
Gave it no further thought, his mind made up for sure.

Abdul asked: "What of Shir and the war?"
And reply: "He will not share conversation, say no more,
He will refrain from asking about your dealings,
As you'll refrain from seeking from him good meanings."

"But we have a new destiny now,
One we share as though of the same brow,
But also different we each are beneath Earth's moon,
You married, me single, and Shir to marry soon."

"Tonight in actual fact,
An Aboriginal with much tact,
Shir has paid his bride price,
And she appears to be very nice."

Nak continued: "You too will grow lonely here,
Nothing to do between jobs, here and there,
You are invited to the wedding of course,
A wedding that Afghan community has decided to endorse."

"But first we must get you sturdy and steady,
A blanket and basic equipment to get you ready,
It can grow cold here during the dark hours of night,
A good blanket will put your weary bones to right."

# AFGHAN

## INTRODUCTION THE SHIR

A great service could be found here in Marree,
And no one could do anything but agree,
For merchandise could be secured for delivery,
And paid for later when wages came flowing like gravy.

It was the culture of the current time,
No prejudice here, no difference between orange and lime,
For the colour of money was the same from each,
From white or from Afghan, money spoke and did not preach.

This place and service was the delivery shed, big business here,
Supplies galore and a service to all, a slogan to adhere,
Bags and sacks of flour, rice, and sugar, an array of stables,
Oatmeal, baking powder, and tea, stacked to roof, no tables.

Items painstakingly ticked off a big list,
A great enterprise that would not desist,
And so here we find Shir as he gathered his sacks and bags,
His shopping list filled as he stood there in near rags.

Shir and Abdul shook hands, each under stare,
Abdul being handsome and Shir as ugly as rear end on mare,
But smile he did for he was happy to no end,
To be wed this night and for loneliness to mend.

Abdul knew nought what to say,
For war talk was banned and he did not wish his mind to stray,
"My time as a cameleer has been varied to vast degree,
But here in Australia I'm sure more to learn there be."

Shir said: "Desert here and desert there,
Ghostly cold by night and peaked at day by sun's glare,
But the colonists are as stupid as stupid can be,
They cannot compete with us, you will surely see."

"We might live in the same town,
But we are the ones steeped in renown,
We command over all transport requirements and need,
Transporting to farmers, supplying all but mead."

"We don't tough alcohol or bacon,
But anything other we are ready to be beckon,
Good reputation with all we have, rigid as a stave,
We are the people's blessing, their mysterious nave."

"We separate ourselves from all those that are late,
And deliver on time, our service is first rate,
We can achieve competitive service cheaper,
And these deals make bartering all the sweeter."

"Once this load is delivered on time as we agree,
We shall transport their wool back to Marree,
But for the minute we must hurry all the more,
For a wedding we attend, for me a great ceremony in store."

# AFGHAN

Nak saw opportunity, good advantage to take,
"Is she a good cook, good meals can she make?"
Shir replied: "She can cook and furthermore still,
A woman of great passion and able to give thrill."

The others laughed at this, happy to hear a joke,
But spiteful looks were cast their way from other bloke,
For let us not forget - of the populace - the racism here,
Always unfortunate and forever in gear.

Shir then said: "Please, come and help me now,
Still work to be done but I am ready to bow,
For the day is drawing to a close,
And I need a wash for I grow on the nose."

Nak to both: "Come and we shall finish up here,
Go to our calling, good company most dear,
Many new friends for Abdul to meet and to talk,
Finish up here and with me come walk."

## WEDDING ARRANGED

Custom in Afghanistan it was for bride price to be paid,
And for this a man's daughter would be laid,
Upon ceremonial pedestal to be wed,
To then be taken most surely by husband to bed.

Time between words of promise and mattress,
Was for the friends and family, alleviate stress,
Each giving their blessings, strong words of steeple,
As newly wedded couple gave cheer to the gathered people.

It was an unfamiliar custom in Australia, this bride price,
Something alluded as though avoiding lice,
But Aborigine had picked up on the custom fast,
For need of money and comfort to last.

A father standing proud with daughter in hand,
To give her up with smile on face as he does stand,
Seeing daughter's hand taken by an Afghan,
Made no difference to the father, of his house, the man.

Where the Afghan was rich with money to spare,
He may be able to capture more than one wife in snare,
Seen more than once this monstrosity,
Men taking advantage of this opportunity.

# AFGHAN

Normal it was for a man to be over sixty,
Taking a wife as young as fourteen, seeing her as sexy,
No crime is it here and so few seemed to care,
But some in society do manage to give a rude stare.

An old man with a dirty mind on child,
Running fingers up one so innocent and mild,
Feeling the inside of her leg for joy,
As though his money for bride price was spent on a toy.

Though never a complaint is heard upon the wind,
For the suffering do so in the raging of their mind,
But Shir was a good man here,
And to one wife he would adhere.

To behold a wife, slightly plump with a little fat,
Saw reflection of eagerness from Afghan with eyes like rat,
Eyes ready to eat, wishing to devour the fish,
Some call this fetish, others prerequisite to be met and to dish.

Further still can we secure more from this time, this decade,
From this century, within the mix of culture and facade,
For Europeans would have little to nothing to do with either,
But Afghan and Aborigine slowly gave to securing good tether.

Times were changing where they saw eye to eye,
Good friends, Aborigine and Afghan, they could seldom deny,
And of the colonists and all they believed in,
They seemingly portrayed little more than to be of great sin.

There was another obstacle in the way, all agree,
Women forbidden to pray in the mosque at Marree,
Men were granted more spiritual comfort which they did expect,
Whilst women were treated to lesser degree, with lesser respect.

Inside the mosque where Shir was to be wed, to verses say,
There was the *mirab* so placed, which faced a certain way,
To Mecca the Koran must be laid in good tradition,
Wrapped and well rested upon place of distinction.

The Koran was treated as a National flag,
Not just any old piece of worn-torn rag,
For no other book was to be placed upon it,
It must have a good station for it was writ.

Shir's wedding would be taken with no less ceremony,
Special custom as though no limit to money,
Shir's wife called Arika, to join him tonight,
To set straight their loneliness, to make things alright.

## THE CEREMONY

In Aboriginal her name meant waterlily, you see,
A name fitting a beautiful wife to be,
Shir was hopeful that his wife was happy and content,
Cared for her, where other men would deny, not allowing consent.

In separate rooms to start out the night,
A *mullah* from Marree to view with delight,
Ensuring all custom was met with alright,
To ensure all ceremony were seamless and tight.

Shir was dressed in *shalwar* trousers, the custom,
Wide at the top and narrow at the bottom,
Largely dissimilar to pantaloons in appearance,
There was a vast amount of difference.

And a turban of white sat upon his head,
Ivory white and of greatest respect,
Arika with dress of white and a veil, musing compassion,
Nothing outlandish but befitting this special occasion.

Arika was comforted in the knowledge of wedlock,
That Shir was a good man who loved her, never to mock,
No unconditional love could she willingly yet give,
But with her new husband she could forever live.

Commit herself to him she would do at will,
Offering goodness to both in their future to fulfil,
Receive great joy from company offered,
Security for life she did hope to be smothered.

To embrace Shir's religion as her very own,
Accustom self to it with maturity grown,
Religion and Afghan were one and the same,
To be married to an Afghan was a religion to claim.

Arika spoke in broken English as best she could,
Shir did the same as expected he should,
For neither knew the others language,
It was a smallish burden, not of real heavy baggage.

And so wed they were amidst all who saw,
Many friends to witness, ceremony of custom and law,
And after good words spoken a feast so huge,
Now married couple, no denying the truth, a new type of refuge.

Showered in blessings from young and old,
*Dalak* of Marree, being happy, from smile be told,
No circumcision her today, he wore another mask,
The *dalak* of Marree performing many a varied task.

The *dalak* was called Zareen,
A man seemingly wealthy and clean,
Bestowing a bow and a gift,
Giving money, good fortune, opposite of rift.

# AFGHAN

Zareen was a lowly man, circumciser of boys,
Also the haircutter most sure, though never annoys,
Only two others exist whom are more lowly then he,
The sieve maker, and a dancer who danced with glee.

"My best wishes to you and new wife,
May your future together prove to be a good life."
"Thank you, Zareen," said Shir smiling and steady,
Despite, in his mind, looking for bed with wife, he was ready.

The assembly was large and hungry, keen for supper,
Many tables of food prepared to stifle much hunger,
Women in veils to which they all adorn well,
Men in their turbans; both sexes, their enthusiasm does swell.

Nak stood before all and gave a short speech,
"I congratulate this new couple, tied together, never to breach,
Please now take to these tables of food, all ready for thee,
Eat all that you can and be content, be as happy as can be."

The throng moved about with great patience,
Never shoving with haste, employing a methodical science,
Conversation thick and most friendly, and to friends rely,
A most hospitable congregation, not a single person could deny.

Shir reflected, most dreamily, on life there ahead,
Upon his wife and the young life she had lead,
Living off the land of the desert, digging out roots like mole,
Amongst forages, creeks, and sparsely strewn water hole.

Amongst rivers and streams, amid the heat,
Where the scorching sun does unkindly beat,
A sun-scorched land which does dry and crack,
And then rainy season and deluge across desert and track.

Shir was so happy, so happy at last,
A beautiful wife, one who mused of character vast,
She was sixteen and he was mighty pleased,
Less than half his age, an ambition of his at last appeased.

Shir was ugly on the outside though handsome on the in,
So lucky he never forced her, he was always without sin,
This was wrought from her personal perspective,
He had also proved to be very protective.

One thought remained, a splinter, a sentence within a tome,
It was time to leave the feast room and to go home,
Time to be man and wife,
Time to begin their new life.

Nak stood before the two, Abdul to his rear,
Both giving free smile and happy they did appear,
"I wish you both the very best, hopefully, even, a little rest,
Tomorrow's work we attend, to work hard and remain the best."

*"Sorry I say, arika, new friend... Ah... new wife,*
*Four weeks gone, we go, but not... no strife,*
*I shall look to Shir for you... whilst go away,*
*Make sure he will not to go... to go astray."*

# AFGHAN

Shir said: "I have some letters for you, for the homestead,
I have to give them to you, but I got distracted instead."
Nak replied: "Do not reflect on it right now,
When we load the camels you can give them a show."

And so Shir and Arika say their good night,
Off they go into the future so bright,
For business is thriving, although very hard,
It is work to last long and never retard.

And in broken English, Arika does speak,
*"All nearly go home, we go to, I think."*
And Shir asked: *"Are you scared for the night?"*
*"No,"* she says, with sincere foresight.

## THE PROSTITUTE

The wedding ceremony is over, good couple new,
Time for Nak to abscond and quench his own desire as it grew,
A secret he keeps to self forever and more,
Only short walk away he does make via misleading tour.

Not too far a prostitute does live,
Of Japanese ethnicity she does give,
Love to those that wish to pay,
For good company as they do lay.

Nak was single and of good moral, good brother,
Though he still had needs as any other,
He deserved love, as per anyone else, without fail,
To feel the warmth of flesh, of a beautiful female.

He was lured more by his loins and his frustration,
A need growing within for great satisfaction,
Wanting to extinguish the desire within,
To accomplish his desire in the midst of his inward grin.

She lived in the Ghantown not that too far away,
Never tempted to find trappings in city, she was here to stay,
For some considered her soul wretched, sinful and worse,
And others a great commodity to be paid for by purse.

# AFGHAN

Her real name was unknown by the community as it stood,
But Saki to those single men of the neighbourhood,
Leading a reasonably pleasant life away from the town centre,
She was seldom seen away from her shelter.

You could not say she was welcomed by the community, her host,
But she provided a service to the men that needed it the most,
And so to men she became accepted for her services here,
Some finding her irresistible, sneaking behind back of all peer.

She had been married once to a wealthy man,
One of Chinese background, and his name was Chan,
He was old and vicious to say the least,
Who had passions for his cook also, he was a snarly beast.

He died not long after being wed to her fast,
He always had her commit to his desires, to the last,
Rough and ready with heavy hand,
With heavy punch to face he always did land.

After his death she had nothing at all,
Caste away like rubbish upon the streets, feeling small,
Nothing left for her and no money to be had,
She was penniless, homeless, cast out, but not mad.

She reinvented herself to be what she is today,
Self-managed and important to those that pay,
Leaving Adelaide behind she found her way here,
To Marree where she carved a new life for her to steer.

She was a prostitute, destined to please,
Nak was a man who had his desires to appease,
His future ambition a secret untold,
To wed Saki and live a life quite bold.

Though she knew nought of Nak's secret untold,
Knew not of his ambition to be so bold,
But she knew and felt his love more than as though kin,
And loving a man like Nak was far short of being a sin.

Nak knew the truth of it all as it stood,
Afghan and Asian was frowned upon by neighbourhood,
Marriage between these two could never be true; never knew,
And so Nak would always feel alone as in older age he grew.

She felt no prejudice for Nak or his religion,
Nak felt no disgust in Saki and her ambition,
He needed love and paid for it here,
She needed funds to secure future year.

He fell upon the shack by a dry creek bed,
Up river, so to speak, so water clean and good health lead,
But little water flowed at this moment in time,
For the heat of the months dried all and left grime.

A few date palms did grow nearby,
A little fruit picked now and then, lullaby,
A clothes line hanging between house and crooked post,
Looking worse for wear but not quite the ghost.

# AFGHAN

Nak passed the clothesline and pulled worn shirt from hanging,
A flag of familiarity meaning that Saki was ready for straddling,
This was her work and those words not meant as disrespect,
For she was a good woman, and to mans' needs never neglect.

He knocked twice upon the door to be certain,
Saw then a shadow moving across window curtain,
Saki opened the door with a smile upon face,
Nak could not reciprocate due to affliction, which is no disgrace.

The outline of her breasts issued great pleasure,
Nak had already, without more, received good measure,
His ill-feelings and pressure was already much less,
Already advantage to spirit and anxiety, and stress.

Her hips and slight plumpness were like heavenly gift,
Enough it was to mend the inner torment and rift,
Nak felt his love for her all the more,
Even without the love making which was yet in store.

Looking each other in the eye,
Saki could never, with Nak, deny,
Taking his hand she lead him straight to bed,
To satisfy his hunger, for him to be fed.

As they stepped Nak spoke a few words as best he could,
"*Good night*," he said, his broken English understood,
"*Yes*," replied Saki as they walked past single lantern,
Past basin, past small cupboard and then did turn.

Facing each other at the foot of the bed,
Nak felt as though he had just been wed,
Saki felt the desire in Nak for sure,
Comfort was present in Nak, no need to lure.

*"I go work, long time, long way,"*
Saki simply smiled, Nak happy and gay,
Nak's grimace and smile ugly to eye,
But she knew that in her Nak did rely.

Nak said: *"I stay long time here,"*
And pulled money from his purse, one held dear,
She pushed it away in order to first fulfil her job,
A duty, a repose, a pleasure to aid, never the snob.

To the night she did tenderly tend,
Kissing softly Nak's grimace, his face, to mend,
Nak's feelings abated, lost in splendour this night,
Here he would stay under morning's first light.

## THE FIRST DREAM OF CONSEQUENCE

This was Char Asiab, 6th October, 1879,
Abdul stood upon the firing line,
Ready to do duty for British here,
Fighting for all he could gain for family this year.

Three British field guns fire from a single ridge,
Firing upon an Afghan position, distance easy to bridge,
British Highlanders, Gurkhas and the 5th Punjab Infantry,
Do what they can to command over this country.

The British lines advance slowly at first,
From the enemy side of fence the scene could not be worse,
The desert explodes in places upon the field, no place to hide,
The noise of battle carrying both far and wide.

Little damage currently seems the effect,
Upon Afghan position whose stronghold mused to be neglect,
And so the gap closes and slows, a faltering tide,
But distance is eventually gained against the defending side.

Both Afghan and British forces litter the ground,
Many dead and wounded around to be found,
Screams from the dying filling the air,
No time to relax or to give a care.

Volley after volley permeates the atmosphere,
The advance continuing now more rapidly does appear,
Battle noise deafening as deafening can be,
Smoke from cannons and weapons as far as the eye can see.

Abdul then woke with a great start and gasping for air,
It has been a long time since bad dream, it just wasn't fair,
But something had jolted his memory from the day before,
Someone he'd recognised, for sure, to be sure.

## PREPARATIONS

The morning broke with the usual ceremonial flare,
Muslim singing, their song, their music blare,
Mystic verses of praise and worship do layer,
Accompanying all as they prepared for prayer.

Afterwards Shir had farewelled his wife of one night,
Abdul departed shed after wrapping turban tight,
Nak arrived last and happy as could be,
No one aware as to where he did flee.

"Good morning to you, Abdul," greeted Shir,
Abdul replies: "A good morning it is, that is for sure,"
"How was your stay in shed, upon bed of hay?"
"The family Bauz were good, comfort I had during my stay."

"And here is Nak, on time again I see,"
"And good morning back," replied Nak, "and to thee,"
To Abdul he had spoken, and Abdul was pleased,
"Thank you Nak, I am refreshed and ready to appease."

Shir said: "All is usually well amongst Afghan swell,
This day is busy and we do all we can to assure we gel,
Each has his place in Ghantown and Marree,
One day you'll see, and will have to agree."

"I already agree," replied Abdul, "of this place,
Friends already I have found, all with profound grace,
This will be a good place to call home, I am sure,
To this friendship, comradery, good cheer, I have bitten a lure."

They had walked over to coral near empty trough,
Their camels waiting, tails waving flies off,
Hardly sun on horizon and already growing hot,
This place in the desert, for the weary it is not.

Nak said to Shir: "You look refreshed after last night,"
"That's because I had a woman to hold me dear and tight,
But where did you go last night, off into the dark?"
"Uh, to see an old friend, and... well... up at first spark."

"And so good company we have all had," Abdul replied to both,
"Each of us rewarded experience to help us in our growth,
For I had good company, shared with the family Bauz,
Greeted this morning with large breakfast on which to gaze."

Shir then started: "We must commence with the deed,
Get these camels from shackle to feed,
Have them packed with goods and ready to move,
For we have a long journey ahead, though little to prove."

Shir then handed a letter to Nak as promised, unread,
"From yesterday, two letters for the homestead."
The last letters to be delivered by hand,
For a small mail service had gripped the land.

# AFGHAN

Jack Hester was his name,
Delivering mail was his game,
Service to grow in conjunction with demand,
A faster delivery than expected across bleakness, across sand.

"I was handed them by the Postmaster late yesterday,
And promised to deliver them without delay."
Nak said: "If they were Muslim, to receive these,
The Postmaster would be slow to appease."

But the Afghans would deliver them regardless of this,
Their manner different than white folk, this you could not miss,
They had nothing to lose by delaying the mail,
Only good reputation and well earned respect upon trail.

Abdul advied with good cheer: "Maybe another order,
Possibly demand for more wool, a job grafted to shoulder,
Bigger rewards and future job, better terms for wage,
A new beginning for you Nak, upon the camel string stage."

There was always room for growth around here,
Good business to receive if to schedule adhere,
Do well to the residents and farmers all,
Gathering more customers meant you would never fall.

Though to work they must get,
If current schedule was to be met,
For loading of stores to camel's back,
Would take time to ready, just a little time to stack.

Abdul was permitted entry to Australia, rather slender,
A three year lease only, a little short and rather tender,
Though administrational records would sometimes disappear,
And longer stay would many appreciated with good cheer.

If Afghan was married, family still overseas, at home,
It was hard to be satisfied with just desert to roam,
Homesickness was part of everyday life,
Especially if at home you had children and wife.

Some would bring family to Australia, sure,
But very few were granted, lacking tackle or lure,
For Australia needed camels and handlers too,
Not children and women with nothing to do.

Many men before Abdul had abandoned their post,
Taken Australia as new home, accept them as host,
Leaving family to perish in Afghanistan and more,
Feeling one selfish ambition, regardless of lore.

No; Abdul was different, his family came first,
He would aid his family, even if worse came to worst,
And the sharpness of knife then hit his heart hard,
In his mind he was totally devoted to wife, to children, his bard.

If denied his family admittance here,
Home he would go, back to family dear,
Whether alive after three years and feeling well,
Or dead as a dormouse and in coffin did smell.

# AFGHAN

Whether wrapped in good clothing or rags,
Dressed real proper or like pauper who nags,
Regardless of circumstance he would return,
To be with his family, family he could never spurn.

Whatever the cost, no matter how dear,
He would serve his time, in Marree, right here,
Even working his fingers to the bone,
He would once more be with family upon throne.

The camel string would soon be ready,
Nose pegs in place and camels steady,
Stores loaded upon the backs of them all,
Ready to depart and see the miles behind them fall.

All were anxious to be on their way,
Camels too needed lifting from demeanour grey,
To trek the land north across scorching land,
Hoping to be free of sandstorm, for sandstorm was banned.

No time here for a delay to hit hard,
So prayer this morning they did for guard,
For safe journey they had all wished,
Hoping for all disaster to be missed.

To homestead they must reach,
Drop off their stores in good manner to teach,
Reload with homestead wool and deliver to station,
Get homestead goods to market, distributed to nation.

The camels were tied in order of advance,
Lead camel to front and kitchen to rear, all to prance,
From Marree to near homestead they would attend,
Just south of Birdsville, a hazardous journey, no friend.

With them one camel, pregnant was she in guise,
To leave behind would be unfair, unwise,
The others would miss her, in heads bells toll,
Camels had great character, like people, with great soul.

More like pets than mountainous features,
Near impossible it was to neglect these creatures,
Each and every camel had its place in the string,
Always they travelled in order, so cheerful as almost to sing.

Each of the three men had eight camels to call his own,
Stick in hand to tame and to direct until familiarity grown,
Each and everyone had a name and characteristic,
Never abuse; never employ against them anger or rude mimic.

Varying colours and sizes and towering tall, a great lump,
Hair growing longest at the shoulder and at the hump,
Dull grey or yellowish brown and yoke,
Main coat colour grey, black, cream, and others just spoke.

White was rare and very seldom was seen,
These animals were family and comrades keen,
An Afghan could never work with a horse,
To do so would fill them with sorrow and remorse.

# AFGHAN

Two Aboriginal boys worked hard and with good grace,
Paid well they were sure never to oneself, disgrace,
They continued to place saddles and supplies where needed,
Much activity undertaken now, as was pleaded.

The boys worked from three lines of stacked merchandise,
With much eagerness they prepared the trip to hell, not paradise,
The Aborigine boys continued to smile as to work they went,
Working systematically they were worth every penny of rent.

Abdul did ask: "To the camels' names, what do you call?"
"That one is Amaroo, and that one Girra, names we have for all,"
Two of the camels, not yet with nose pegs in place,
Did change positions within the string, they seemed to race.

These animals knew their place well,
Understood formalities and in them pride does swell,
They had their own minds which worked like well-oiled gear,
"It's only the lazy ones that need a whisper in ear."

"Never hit hard with your stick or readily provoke,
They take to their jobs superbly, that is no joke,
Very seldom you need to hit them hard,
Most will bend to your will and you will be their guard."

Nak looked at the eight under his command,
Gave an order and all stood as was demand,
Abdul then tried and only two stood,
The other six were as though made of wood.

"They are testing you, Abdul, that's all,
Show them who's boss, shoulders back, stand tall,
Bark out your order and make them react,
They will adapt quickly to your voice and your tact."

And so formalities of the early morning proceeds,
Familiarity for animals and men, fulfilling their needs,
Three men and two Aboriginal boys under occasional gaze,
Toiling away under the growing heat and the blaze.

The front-most camel of each eight camel string,
Had a riding saddle attached for rider to sit as though king,
A saddle of two forks, one in front and one behind,
Leather-covered seat, with stirrups, secure mind.

The camels worked hard for the men as though seemingly agreed,
In return they must attend the camels everyday need,
Constantly checking for sores on camels back,
Checking lashings, and straps, every tack.

Pack saddled may require relining with jute,
Strong fibre from wool bales to remedy, camel discomfort mute,
Unmuzzled camels may require muzzling at times during ride,
Temperamental dispositions seeing one bite another's hide.

They were a team like no other,
Men and camels: camel the worker and men the mother,
Saddles refilled with straw through small slits,
Which overtime turned to chaff, hence replacing with straw bits.

# AFGHAN

Saddle sores could become infested,
Where infection would be nested,
Fly-blown lesions that caused death,
A worrying sight able to stall one's breath.

Feet too needed to be constantly checked and scrutinized,
To be free of abrasions and cracks, washed and sterilized,
Cameleers loved their camels to the very last,
Like family they were, as though of family cast.

The loads sitting upon a camel's back,
Seemingly stable and resting upon solid rack,
Although sometimes sway from side to side during the move,
Always taken from them at night, delicately removed.

Thongs and cordage were tied secure,
Allowing for quick adjustment and removal to cure,
For unstable loads upon camel was annoying at best,
Quick to hurt and rub, and forced upon string unnecessary rest.

Nose peg of hardwood was connected to each camel,
No need for a bit in mouth like horse to travel,
String attached from peg to other camel's rear,
An easier way to maintain discipline and to steer.

The connection sagged in the middle with ample room spare,
No pain evident unless camel tried to bolt from his snare,
No heat-conducting metal employed for use as these,
For cameleers were fond of their camels, each to appease.

Camels worked hard for their owners, sturdy stock,
The cameleers protected and served these beasts of rock,
Each relied on the other for good life,
Any other form of existence would cause strife.

As packs of merchandise was stowed,
The cameleers fondled their friends, eyes glowed,
Quiet word from cameleers lip,
Deep throaty grown reply or responsive nip.

Playful they are, capable of dry eye or tear,
Own persona each has and matured each year,
If only they could talk it would be a great friendship,
Their disposition one could never dissect or strip.

Everything to love and nothing to hate,
Always on time and never late,
Happy to trudge the extra mile per day,
Before napping at night under stars without hay.

Another easily seen here was the kitchen camel,
Always last in line, in the order of travel,
Water and food, pots and pans clanging about,
Utensils, cups and bowls, all that men could not go without.

Abdul looked into the eye and then upper lip of one,
The camel reminding him of a story long gone,
It was a story of how they did silently move,
And had come about the lip which bear a small groove.

# AFGHAN

How Muhammad had kissed the lip of a camel,
And since that day hare lips did they have, wherever they travel,
It was a gift from Muhammed to all descendent,
All creatures of this type did display, loudly and most strident.

In little under forty minutes all told,
They were ready to move, content and bold,
The sun had risen above the horizon, moon now tired,
Time to get moving, only one other thing required.

Nak had a rifle, help in crook of arm, you see,
For Al Halal meat was forever available in Marree,
But once out on the sand and running low on food,
For good meat all three may be in the mood.

In the Ghantown where they live,
It is easy to take and to give,
But it is the *mullah* that resides here,
And to him a responsibility for which to adhere.

Adhere to religious law,
Never to flaw,
Always to abide,
Never to wash out with tide.

The guidelines were explained in the Koran,
Everyone knew it, every single man,
Meat was gained by using a sharp knife,
Killing animals whilst still full of life.

Dragging sharp edge over jugular vein,
Blood to come oozing from the artery main,
Then allowed to bleed and die in their sight,
As butcher did accomplish what he believed right.

Long strips of salted meat that Nak had available,
May run out during journey leaving none for table,
This would mean slaughtering a kangaroo or other,
Preparing meat so that hunger they could smother.

Whilst facing Mecca, regardless of how far,
Nak would recite, 'Bismillah Wallahu Akbar',
Sacrifice to Allah is what this does entail,
Whilst animal dies and whines and sometimes thrashing his tail.

But die it must not before conclusion of prayer he did reach,
Animal to suffer as the *mullah* does make his grand speech,
Applying this verse to his one and only God,
He then proceeds as though given the nod.

If the animal dies before prayer is complete,
Leave the animal to rot there at his feet,
So thinking of this he checked his weapon once more,
Prior to placing it away upon saddle, in bag to store.

No sooner than done and they were to farewell their stay,
Camels stood up and they were upon their way,
A long journey ahead but they would return back home,
The Ghantown falling behind them and much desert to come.

## OF THE CAMEL

The noble dromedary that Nak had in his string,
Were descendants of India, descendants of king,
Trustworthy and sometimes witty, hard workers and fast,
No lazy bone amongst them, hard workers to the very last.

The camel could go two to three weeks without water,
Glory be, a grand total of abstinence and no slaughter,
Able to drink twenty gallons of fluid at a single sitting,
Able to go so long without drink for a camel is fitting.

The heat of the Australian sun,
For the most part was simple and fun,
Forty degrees in the shade of the coolest tree,
They were simply content and happy with glee.

So much better than a horse or an ox,
Higher than both, tall and witty as fox,
Spinifex never concerned a camel in any way,
So high up they did clear, no damage to stay.

The assortment of goods carried in sacks,
Upon backs and side saddles with glistening tacks,
Nothing was harmed by spinifex at all,
Because, yes, that's right, they were so very tall.

Tell-tale signs of camels having passed by,
Hair upon spinifex does not lie,
Legs three foot long they move through scrub and turf,
Their skin as black and hard as rock on earth,

Their skin becomes as hard as iron rails,
A horse being torn to shreds, it all pales,
For significance is in the breeding,
So why bring horses into a place not needing.

Spinifex, a plant to aid in erosion,
A notorious plant having spread like explosion,
And small birds and animals use the plant wise,
Aboriginals have their uses and weapons to devise.

Saltbush country edged with mulga, as like the shore of sea,
Undulating sandhills as far as the eye can see,
Rabbit burrows infesting the ground,
Easy to see as you look all round.

Plenty of meat here as can be relied,
Dingo, emu, kangaroo, all can be abide,
A single shot from a rifle and it is ready to treat,
A meal to dress, a meal to eat.

But wound the animal Nak would have to try,
Otherwise allowed to rot, and meat for them it would deny,
Religion is religion and in it they trust,
Without it they would simply turn to rust.

# AFGHAN

And mulga was a good meal for a camel and more,
And against all belief no water in hump does he store,
A camel will absorb the fat from within, a supplementary dish,
The hump falling short and to slowly diminish.

The animal could extract moisture well,
Taking much from mulga and paracelis to aid in dry spell,
Their pads were soft, best for moving over sand,
Quite often the string would avoid heavily trodden land.

Soles hard to take the heat,
Seemingly cushioned and very neat,
Made for hard work, hard labour,
This beast was a legend of all land and Nullarbor.

Uncanny sense of direction and good memory in store,
Knowing where they are going if been there before,
Three miles an hour for up to ten hours a day,
Though stand still in one spot too long and they say nay.

Seeing some sign out of the ordinary would grasp attention,
They would look and stare in that general direction,
Memory with them all of the time to stay,
For next time coming past they look for that sign in the same way.

They were quite remarkable,
They were very, very able,
They were polite and worked as hard as the heart,
They were good friends, never to part.

## THE FIRST DAY

They had been moving along at good pace for some hours,
When Nak looked to his camel, Chocolate, who towers,
High above Nak the camel does peer and stare,
Ahead of him something... moving upon track, amidst glare.

Ah, Chocolate, Nak's favourite beast of all owned,
Each camel in his 8-camel string did seem to atone,
For they were all yellowish brown with dark mane,
Everyone and each of semblance they did maintain.

So Nak followed the camels gaze,
And sees a figure upon the shimmering maze,
Seemingly seated in shade not far up ahead,
Looked similarly Aboriginal, his stature easily read.

They came upon him soon enough, quite close,
Passing him by seeing infliction quite gross,
A victim of his mother's cruelty, no joke,
His lips burnt away from face, with hot embers she did poke.

Nak and Shir had seen him before,
Upon this land on occasion he does explore,
Holding his hands out for a morsel of meat,
But little does the string have to allow him to eat.

# AFGHAN

A sorrowful sack of bone,
Little real flesh, no body tone,
A shell of emptiness and very weary,
His eyes peering up but looking rather bleary.

His name was forgotten, he was a wanderer of sorts,
Forever on walkabout, or so go the reports,
From a distance he appears happy with smile on face,
But closer, you'll see, bare teeth a disgrace.

No lips to close over mouth forever more,
Mother's torture, bad treatment they deplore,
A punishment inflicted when he was a very young boy,
When he played with his foul dinner as though a toy.

An alcoholic mother of bad spirit and soul,
No sense of pity or remorse, but upon him a toll,
Picking up hot stick from burning ember,
Strike hard until burnt this family member.

But that is the way it is here in the bush,
No one to rush out with aid, just remain hush,
A sadness to see this was pure evil itself,
Something unable to be put from mind, put to shelf.

And then further on another is seen,
Half-caste for sure and extremely unclean,
Neglected and thrown like rubbish about,
No home, no one to say 'come', no one to shout out.

Pasted over the land like freckles on face,
These people discarded as though a disgrace,
No one wants them hanging around anywhere near,
They are called pests of society and all do sneer.

This one here would sell herself short,
Give her body to some white man for good sport,
To be paid a pittance for something to eat,
No family around, no one to greet.

Abdul was the last string, was last in line,
To see soon enough, cold shiver creeping up spine,
He had come here to make money, for family and security,
To send home all he could, yes indeed, a surety.

He had served the great British Empire,
And Australia was part of that which he did aspire,
But the more he did see of this land,
The more he grew ashamed of all he'd played of his hand.

So they continued on their way,
Much time available later to have one's say,
As they moved along, pot and pans continued clanging,
Metallic melody teasing the hungry, and the utensils hanging.

## FODDER

The day was commencing to draw to a close,
And time for prayer, time to grasp, to attain repose,
The camels required feeding and so did all men three,
Nourishment provides much strength and the body does agree.

Beautiful reds and oranges spanning the land,
Many colours and hues enough to make a man stand,
Stop walking about and look all you can: feel cheer, feel healthy,
This view is for free and a sight most worthy.

The way and effort in securing good grazing land here,
Was for the cameleers to be wary of land up front and rear,
Always looking for good place to set up camp,
Forcing the camels to not wander off and upon country tramp.

A fine shallow, an old creek bed, sits as though fallow,
Bush and trees and grass yellow,
Everything here needed for a hungry camel to snack,
Just wait for the packs to be removed from each back.

Camels are position, each string of eight aside,
Packs to be removed from  their position astride,
Forelegs folded down towards the ground,
Followed by rear legs onto hindquarters as mound.

Thongs and cordage, tacks unfastened too,
Allowing packs easy removal, there was much to do,
Working remarkably fast and Abdul under watchful eye,
He was found to be working tirelessly, no one could deny.

The two front legs were tied by rope shackle,
Nothing the camel with teeth could tackle,
Short hobbles applied to all in their presence,
And let the camels loose to feed, not restricted by fence.

Nose pegs untied to allow free reign for all,
The kitchen unpacked but never let fall,
Much activity to conduct and much to achieve,
Before night was too cold and the flies did all leave.

Each camel knew its place in the line,
Could smell his pack as though rats to lime,
The camels would know where to straddle,
In readiness in morning for replacement of saddle.

Not too far out will they stray,
Most will remain near their masters whom near fire stay,
Hindered by shackle, this restraint good and proper,
To go more than a mile away they would not bother.

When night fell it fell erratically fast,
The heat from the day escaping as though from vacuum blast,
A fire built eagerly for something to eat,
But religious commitment comes before sustenance and meat.

# AFGHAN

Another moon was expected tonight,
It would provide some very decent light,
But until then all three should work fast,
Get everything sorted before the light was at its last.

## THE FIRST CAMP

The camp was relatively easy to appease their need,
The night possibly colder than any other, would not impede,
A campfire for cooking was second important to all,
Second to prayer, from which they would never stall.

They had already placed there sleeping covers and sheet,
Folded up into tight rolls and ready to meet,
And with nearly everything completed,
The Koran was revealed to which all eyes greeted.

Nak was *jemadar* and responsibility was his to be graced,
So with this in hand and prayer mat placed,
He prepared to read the most appropriate,
For their needs and thoughts, for their new associate.

Ablutions should to be conducted in the usual manner,
It was very important and it really did matter,
Five pillars there are here,
Five times per day to recite amidst silent cheer.

But this was the dilemma for cameleers,
They could not do the same as all of their peers,
They could not waste water amidst  the desert shades of red,
And so sand they employed in its stead.

# AFGHAN

Small piles of sand sat beside them each,
A semblance of water but ritual they could preach,
They would perform their duties as good men should,
Just not in the proper way in which it was understood.

Five pillars were also altered,
They could not pray as so ordered,
Salat-al-Fajr, Salat-al-Zuhr, Salat-al-Ast they were,
Salat-al-Maghrib and Salat-al-Isha great emotions stir.

Sunrise, noon, afternoon, sunset and night could not be,
So drop the afternoon and night it was decree,
Longer they would spend during times of other,
To make up for lost prayer and hope for forgiveness from brother.

And one further degree,
In which we sometimes see,
For Nak on occasions sees Salat-al-Zuhr given leave,
The sun was too hot at that hour, which sees each man grieve.

## RESPECTFUL NIGHT

The light from the fire lifted the cheer of the men, of all of them,
Faces appeared happy and from this goodness did stem,
They sat cross-legged with mug of tea,
Not a cloud in the sky, they felt as though toil free.

The cold of the night would fall, as cattle herded from croft,
No cloud cover to cover them from aloft,
No cloud cover to keep the heat in by night,
Good need there was to wrap up tight.

The brightness of stars high above,
Was something to easily provide your love,
The Milky Way seen clearly as it spanned the night sky,
So picturesque and clear, enough to make a grown man cry.

Stars winking as though breathing in and out,
No denying that God was mighty, there was no doubt,
It was sheer beauty on a scale worthy to view,
Something bold and grand, all contemplation just grew.

It cast memories to fall upon the mind,
Recalling old friends, some simple, some kind,
Memory of times upon this great earth,
In other countries, in particular the one of your birth.

# AFGHAN

And of vulnerability did come to thought,
Of the vastness about and no other company to be sought,
So peaceful and quiet, as quite could be,
Where wind was still and solitude alone did spree.

Where they had stopped there was nothing at all,
Not even the telegraph wire above them so tall,
They had moved away from the beaten track, and,
The camels found it easier to move on soft sand.

Away and aside from the telegraph wire,
Gave each man and camel a clearer desire,
No reminder to see how far travelled,
No mark in mind to be chiselled.

Instead they employed landmarks to appease their need,
Vast sweeping plains and hills gift knowledge as though to feed,
Creek lines and familiar large trees give sign,
These signposts in which their minds did design.

Clever thinking during long journeys to last,
Across dry land which seemed so bare and vast,
Better to trek without telegraph line overhead,
Solitude delivered and inwards bred.

Shir added the finishing touches to their meal,
Nak took Abdul for short walk to conviction appeal,
For his need was for Abdul to do as they did,
Regardless of trust in him which had already been bid.

To check on the camels one last time before, to sleep, fall,
Familiarise Abdul with the characteristics of all,
Camel's and their company the lifeblood of all they did inhibit,
All preferred camel than man for company though did not admit it,

So the sun had drawn to a close upon most temporary home,
The seemingly short day from time sun did come,
Very busy it was indeed and all would agree to tell,
But time for a short story before eyelids declared farewell.

Nak began his story after briefly setting the scene about,
Of Aborigine people, small tribe of these parts no doubt,
The fire flickering a melody to reflect his tone,
Devastation as it come to nest, seemingly placed upon throne.

Viciousness and Aborigine were of the same word,
Nothing to part them, they were of the same herd,
It is evil to speak of these things since passed, not paltry,
But Abdul needed to know the truth of this sunburnt country.

A husband did look down upon the face to spurn,
A creature of the opposite sex, ready to burn,
A creature of the incorrect sex, one to neglect,
For the tribe needed a man, take this one as a mark of disrespect.

The disgust upon the man's face was painted clear for all,
Never hid his emotion did he, but allow it to fall,
He felt no connection with this person, this baby so thin,
This child his own flesh that he did not see as kin.

# AFGHAN

He picked her up by the feet and swung her real fast,
Bashing her head against rock as was his task,
The brain splattering everywhere you care to look,
The mother sobbing frantically as terror, to soul, had shook.

The sorrow within her was like a tidal wave true,
How this had come about she had little clue,
But some men are strange in a land of hard living,
For them it is hard for love to be giving.

No final hug or warning had the mother received,
No time for her to prepare, nothing left on which to grieve,
Her life had just been ended in the flash of an eye,
Her child's life taken from her, good life to deny.

The husband scolded the wife and kicked her hard,
Kicked the mother as though piece of filth from shoe to discard,
Not a shred of empathy lingering about,
No feeling in him of guilt to give shout.

He took the body and disappeared from sight,
Taking limp body, being denied proper cremation right,
He then built a small fire to burn the body away,
Not wanting the flesh and bones on earth to stay.

But the fire would not start and kept going out,
No matter what he did it just wouldn't flare out,
And in short manner of time the smell of blood on the air,
Did bring dingoes galore out of their lair.

And so throw the body down the man did do,
The dingoes rushing in and ripping apart, devouring raw stew,
Some taking a piece of the body away,
For it to remain a part of the land to this very day.

How did the cameleer know this was true,
How could he be sure that in it the truth grew,
For word of mouth it terribly sound and does solidly stand,
Spoken well from one to another across forsaken land.

No writing instruments or other way to communicate,
No messenger at door or solid oak gate,
No history books to fall upon for lesson to learn,
All is verbal and truth spoken in good turn.

Abdul wasn't sure of the point of the story,
Found it to be a little too gory,
But it reminded him of what he had seen earlier today,
And understood viciousness to be part of the Aboriginal way.

Aboriginal people, though sacred they are, so Abdul learnt,
Mused to have a harsh life in this land so burnt,
Their laws and way of life so different than any other,
Afghan or white man, the Aborigine was satanic, tougher.

Nak had meant it as no rebuff for Shir,
Whose own wife at home seemed to be heavenly pure,
But reflect on the story just spoke he did, not scoff,
Something to contemplate and would be hard to be rid of.

# AFGHAN

And so the slumber of night is now to take place,
Nothing further of the day to embrace,
Shir to dream of wife, and Nak of Mungerannie Gap,
Abdul of his time on the British line with rifle held by strap.

## THE SECOND DREAM OF CONSEQUENCE

A shockingly loud bang filled the air, red flashes of light off glare,
Abdul then saw a soldier hurled backwards, unaware,
His legs torn from torso, feet from limb,
Abdul's possible future, it made him feel grim.

But push on he did towards the enemy now,
Ready to take life and he knew just how,
And he saw a man's head appear up ahead,
The smile upon the face of the enemy easily read.

A soldier behind fortification with grin on face,
A beautiful smile for which to embrace,
The enemy enacting kills upon the field,
The battle around, open, little to no shield.

The man was taking shots at British as they did appear,
No thought to retire, no contemplation to fall to rear,
An enemy of strong conviction and resolution,
He was intent to stay and fight, his only solution.

'Praise Allah,' Abdul heard upon the breeze, it did astound,
Unbelievable to think in the battle noise around,
The smiling man again aiming over rifle sight,
To take another life from the British fight.

# AFGHAN

Abdul realised them that the gun fire had slowed,
The British behind him had momentarily been stowed,
This was not good for being on the front line,
No fire support, life harder to preserve: "Please preserve mine."

He then fired automatically at another target ahead,
Unsure really but in mind a target was read,
A puff of smoke filling before his eyes and to temporarily blind,
He shot up in bed, to a new day not yet ripe, his second to grind.

## THE GATHERING

When morning broke it was met by three men waking,
Blankets stowed and readied for final packing,
The most important of tasks was met, the grandest priority,
Ablutions and prayer having secured their notoriety.

As Shir took to preparing breakfast the others went to task,
Seeking out camel and herding them, no need to ask,
There was also the checking of stores, essential mapping,
Checking of saddles and all manner of strapping.

Few birds there are to greet the morning activity,
Where flies commence the annoyance in life of brevity,
Though sounds can be heard they are seldom allocated,
All part of the chorus, of the song of the desert so associated.

This was the hour of birth given to light of day,
A gift to the morning from all creatures that lay,
Hidden from view but all appearing to be gay,
Always to be heard and part of the play.

Other sounds could be heard upon the light wind and afore,
A storm in far, far distance, a hundred miles away or more,
And regardless of this grand music to ear,
It was silent and calm, atmosphere enough to bring on a tear.

# AFGHAN

The camels are relatively easy to find,
As with mouths busy, their food they grind,
Bells on necks giving their general locations away,
Affixed the night before, prevents them going too far astray.

Within a half mile of campsite,
It was quick and easy to put string back to right,
Chocolate found by Shir and used as a lure,
Many camels following his lead, their leader most sure.

They had eaten the night before,
Good sleep and then eat some more,
Ready for a hard day's travel ahead,
Their heads held high, contented moods easily read.

Abdul confided in Shir so as not to impede Nak,
But he was feeling the isolation, wishing for home, to be back,
"I feel the weight of it upon my shoulders,
My desire for my family, forever embers within me, it smoulders."

"I feel the weight of it here every day,
The feelings are detrimental to my stay,
I don't wish to burden Nak with my quandary,
My family comes first, not secondary."

"I must be here to earn for family's sake,
But being away is like being hit with toothed rake,
I cannot win for whatever I decide,
I feel I am casting my family aside."

Says Shir: "It is true, to be sure,
The love of family, sincere and pure,
But look to the bright side if you may,
Only three years here and then forever with family stay."

"Do not think too much on it, heed not the misery you take,
Just think on the work ahead and the money you'll make,
Your wife and children will flourish ever more for your sacrifice,
For all you do here your life will be all the better and very nice."

"I suffered too," continued Shir,
Feeling as though stuck, forever a pessimistic mure,
"And Nak too has his facial affliction,
But he has forced for himself a solid conviction."

"It is all the same to us now, no essential cure,
We simply do what we must in order to secure,
Our futures grace and temperance,
To have a grand future, a deliverance."

"You will get used to the condition and the loneliness,
Never give your future a second guess,
What lays ahead of you is paved in gold,
For you and family to grow, graceful and bold."

"When in Marre you will find community and friends,
To stand by you no matter what your trends,
We are like brother and sister forever,
Caring for one and then for the other."

# AFGHAN

"But you won't be spending much time in Marree,
We are going to work, all three of us as did agree,
Time will go fast, fast as can be,
Three years will be the blink of an eye, you'll see."

Abdul said: "You are right and it is agreed,
I need to stop negative feeling, which to mind I feed,
But what else to think on, when on the road?
Nothing all day but mile after mile of desert abode."

"That is hard to answer,
Harder still to master,
For each day will be different,
Depending on many, varied predicament."

"Some days are like a year spent,
Others less than a few seconds lent,
Depends on if something does occur,
Or how well trained your mind is to administer cure."

Abdul said in contemplation,
"I suppose it is a simple negation,
Refuse this place and length of each day,
Take them in stride and consider what future lay.

Shir replied: "And that is your answer true,
Another perspective, something new,
Regardless of this you will find a way,
And in three years time you'll consider it a short stay."

## THE MISSIONARY

Loading a string of camels was done so in reverse,
Harder than unloading and considered by some a curse,
It was a challenge on occasion for it was strenuous indeed,
For camels could not rest fully loaded regardless of mans' need.

Shir reached for his water canteen,
To quench his thirst he was keen,
His last drink for quite some time,
Water discipline self taught, pristine, prime.

Bells and hobbles to remove,
Nose pegs placed above lip with groove,
Ready to stand the team as one,
Single command ushered in tone.

Standing on hind legs first and straighten them now,
Front legs opened at knees, forequarters raised, camels from bow,
Push forward onto one front leg and then the next,
Up and ready for the day to come, perfect action as written in text.

The camp now clear of their stay that night,
Time for the journey, time to take flight,
Eight to ten hours more, no real delight,
But the song of the desert will appease, devoid of fright.

# AFGHAN

They stepped off one foot in front of the other,
Much distance ahead, their tracks, grains of sand does cover,
Taking seconds, minutes and hours by stride,
Abdul does all he can to allow feelings to strategy abide.

There are places enroute, for camel, that allow for easier going,
It is all in the knowledge of area, all in the knowing,
Avoid the easy accept the extreme, fewer horse teams on the track,
And to all degree, avoid the bullocks of the outback.

Not long on the road north and Nak saw something ahead,
Immediately familiar it was and even in the heat easily read,
Chocolate looked up and voiced his opinion, too,
For what they saw was something they both knew.

The silhouette of a man beside covered wagon,
The blemishing waves of heat, mirage, try and imagine,
But no mistaking this, it was easy to decipher, and on guess rely,
No question about it, no need to deny.

Chocolate though was a little confused, not ignorant,
For the last time he saw this was somewhere different,
Though familiarity of image was there to test,
His memory as for humans was always his commodity best.

Nak gave warning to those that followed behind,
"Missionary ahead," a man of sacred mind,
Abdul looked up from the rear, his eyes did strain,
Saw the shimmering picture, pixels, coloured grain.

As the gap between the two diminished,
It was easier to see what could never be missed,
A man of God though of different belief,
The three Muslims only hoped for passing to be brief.

Brother Johann Ernst Jakob [Jacob] was the man's name,
Known far and wide, temperament tame,
A bullock team under control of whip, his sway,
Tails moving to flay flies from buttocks away.

He was walking beside the team,
His body not muscular, rather lean,
Having a short stretch of both leg,
As he went along his way, aiding all, and those that beg.

The Brother of Christian [Lutheran] religion,
On the road every day of the year preaching to legion,
Walking his team or travelling upon wagon seat,
Only stopping on occasion for something to eat.

To and from Port Augusta he did travel,
Supplying the mission at Killalpaninna, a desert naval,
The mission provided a service of religion, to all those around,
To provide good service to men and women of religion found.

For Johann the needless journeys across desert plains and bays,
Were coming to the end of their steaming hot days,
For the train and Marree meant there was far less work to be done,
More time for him to preach, so really he had won.

# AFGHAN

Killalpaninna Mission, first decided in January, 1867,
Missionaries having first arrived as though gift from heaven,
Having settled out from Langmeil, never to stall,
Three and a half months after, arrive upon desert, all.

Killalpaninna was not too far ahead,
Possibly 25 miles out from of Cooper Creek bed,
Out-stations Kopperamanna and Etadunna Station,
Incorporated into what was Bethesda Mission.

Johann appeared to recognise Nak,
Gave nod of the head as he lightly whipped bullocks' back,
"May God be with you, brothers, let him build an altar within,
Release you of the savagery of your belief, being forever in sin."

Nak understood little of what was said,
Not purely for English spoken, but slight German accent bred,
And so, "*Allah be with you*," was returned first rate,
Spoken with sincerity and not with hate.

The calling of Allah struck Johann hard,
But reflected not, his mellow smile his guard,
Whether two friends or enemies it mattered not,
They treated each other with respect, right there on the spot.

## COOPERS CREEK

Cooper Creek could be allusion,
Cooper Creek could carry confusion,
Spin off from Cooper could be Cooper or rot,
Was creek to their front Cooper or not.

So vast the names and system about,
Cooper Creek so known where trees give sprout,
What other creek could it be,
Not for anyone to guess or disagree.

Cooper Creek was around these parts, yes,
But was this to their front right now, just guess,
Call it Cooper for Afghan was not sure,
But which other could it be, a grand animal lure.

Many years of summer sees the creek dry,
And at others it is running though slow, as though shy,
From Queensland to north, a possible flood,
Flowing down through NSW to south, like veins of blood.

Regardless of the situation found,
To this beauty they were all bound,
Endowed by 3.5 miles of expansive floodplain,
Though hard to decipher from ground, confusion one does gain.

# AFGHAN

Water was here and creek full of life,
Shadows flickering and flirting, relaxing, little strife,
Fishes and birds, and amphibian life here,
Lucky you'll be if large fish with eyes above water does peer.

The camels would have smelt the water long before,
Though little they would need due to what earlier they store,
Walking leisurely they tenderly approach,
Afghans at their side and ready to coach.

Picturesque as the scene was there would be no respite,
Nak didn't want the camels to lose all for which they did fight,
The camels would grow lazy if given a drink at every stop,
Lazy camels opposed to tough and cream of the crop.

Many Europeans fed water to camels every three days,
Nothing but deterrent and honestly wicked in their ways,
Offering easy way out and never the tough,
Made lazy camels, harsher times rendered rough.

Allowing a camel to water every ten days is finely tuned,
This may procure a total of 20 days when desperate, well pruned,
Water discipline it is and needed to be taught,
A well worn and trained camel was better than distraught.

Call it water fatigue or stress,
Call it what you need, call it a mess,
Treat kindly but harsh,
From desert to marsh.

No matter the climate or predicament,
Good training is rudiment,
Without such training,
Dead camels come raining.

Sixteen to twenty gallons in a single sitting,
If a camel drinks less than it is spoilt by constant filling,
Longer stretches in between is the need,
Water for camels is far different than feed.

Camels are ships of the desert forever more,
Afghans good handlers able to administer as any choir,
Knowledge of surroundings go hand in hand,
Such knowledge sought from Aborigines that walk the land.

Every precaution, all of the time,
Moulding good camel, condition most prime,
Never sway from good training true,
Never underestimate a camels' ability to do.

Nak said: "We don't stop, keep them on the move,
The camels will drink if opportunity does prove
Take a quick mouthful with cup of hand,
Feed yourself, though, by rule to camel we stand."

Abdul said: "A good place to stop and pray."
Replies Nak: "We cannot change our routine today,
Think of the camels and their training we must,
Do not allow them to drink or in future they rust."

# AFGHAN

"Allah knows we are loyal to him, always to follow and do,
To his beliefs we adhere, we are consecrated and true,
Water is weak and these camels are strong,
To gift them water opportunities is very, very wrong."

The creek depth before them was rather unknown,
So for first time at journey their bodies were upon saddle thrown,
Now straddling the camels the cameleers did ride,
So high above ground, so high astride.

With supplies piled high and far from ground,
Portage goods never exposed to water found,
960 pounds of maximum weight, and more if desired,
Always maintained and convictions never retired.

These were camels and part of a string,
Not caravan or wagons pullers with supplies to bring,
Wagons unless built high were not that great,
They too were subject to gifting supplies in wet state.

Abdul cupped his hand and help it extremely low,
Gifting water to mouth, feeling refreshed, a pleasant glow,
The moisture running the length of his throat,
Like water cascading into dry castle moat.

It was tasty and refreshing,
Naturally good and a blessing,
It was like being in heaven above,
Less the seventy-two virgins to love.

Within minutes the string was across,
"Check their nose peg," yelled Nak, their boss,
"Sometimes they are broken,"
Task already done, even as spoken.

Not much to it, not much at all,
No need to slow, no need to stall,
No need to rest, no need for prayer,
No need to refresh camels amidst water's glare.

## NATTERANNIE SANDHILLS

These first four days of travel was a peak, a best,
No flogging dead horse, no putting camels to test,
Simply pushing alone at great pace,
Across land for ten plus hours a day they did trace.

Ahead were the Naterannie Sandhills,
Gorgeous ridges of hue likes grills,
In some places like snakes upon the lands,
Ridges of assorted colour bands.

A wedge-tailed Eagle then caught Abdul's eye,
Magnificent species flying so high,
Wings of fortitude help out upon brightness of sky,
Silently glide, black, long, mysterious, he could not deny.

Diamond-shaped tail,
Talons sharper than any nail,
Chestnut coloured nape,
Unmistakable in shape.

Some parts of the country were appealing but bleary,
Filled with beauty but also quite eery,
So peaceful and quiet, serine,
Bitter and vicious, obscene.

No clear cut way to put it,
A land of own desire and wit,
Characteristics battling against one another,
Life-giving to some but life-taking from other.

Gorges and hills with peak,
Steep hills of high volume they speak,
Low lands flat as can be,
Many contrasts around to see.

But for some it was too much,
Seeing it all the time now failed to touch,
No inner warmth felt by Nak,
And Shir was also quick to turn his back.

Only Abdul saw the raw beauty of land and sky,
Of the country around and all he could spy,
Many weeks and months had the others suffered,
They were not impressed by what was offered.

Nak and Shir must have minds of steel,
What did they think of during stretch from meal to meal,
Long stints of nothing to do but walk,
No opportunity except at night to talk.

Day after day was always the same,
Seemingly nothing to do but play the game,
Working and toiling hour after hour,
What did the mind receive regarding stimulating shower?

# AFGHAN

Australia seemed better than Afghanistan, but only just,
Fortune would be a long time coming though in it he trust,
He contemplated Jehangir in Port Augusta aiding another,
Even so many miles apart he gave to Nak as though mother.

Abdul had a stomach full of food,
Friends who always appeared in good mood,
A working day that kept him busy at toil,
No time to spend allowing laziness to soil and spoil.

Much unemployment there was in reality here,
Long lines in queue and much scrutiny from unkindly leer,
And in Afghanistan it was even worse, especially with wife,
Being poorly and grovelling upon soil to sustain life.

A man made his life at best he could,
Took the best offer as he should,
Always there was fruit upon the tree,
Ready to pick, branches to move and you'll see.

Carve your own future,
No time to wait for a caring nurture,
Appease yourself and your own need,
No one else will aid you with such greater speed.

But continue on regardless of mind's lay,
Past Mulka to Mungerannie for another day,
Mungerannie is Aborigine for 'big ugly face',
A name that holds very little grace.

## MUNGERANNIE

Do not pass into view of the town,
It is as many with white trash acting the clown,
Cursing and blasting their hatred of race,
A short cut would also offer better pace.

It is not just the Afghans that the population hate,
Though they take jobs from many by offering cheaper rate,
But the camels which they believe hideous in every way,
Wishing only that in Afghanistan the camel would stay.

But how hard was it for the idea to sink in,
To replace their frowns with a deep grin,
For white trash  here to take heed and discard ideas vintage,
To rear the camel themselves, properly and to great advantage.

To be looked upon disgustingly by the wives of the men,
A cold stare that could kill before the count of ten,
An ungodly glare to Afghan and more,
And of every Aborigine they do deplore.

It was here that Abdul was gifted a lesson,
They were at a junction of deserts, the Simpson,
Tirari, Sturt and Stony, amidst dry air,
And mention of the Strzelecki Desert just to be fair.

# AFGHAN

Sheer solitude and quiet no matter where you look,
Except that song of the desert which penetrated every nook,
Many variety of bird life crying for water holes and spring,
Calling to young and mates, reverberating calls sing.

Many, many species can be counted about,
So many varieties of birdlife each gifting a shout,
The next generation of life just waiting,
Or hatched already and looking for the season of mating.

But for the most the desert plains around,
Were just that, flat and barren ground,
Emptiness seemingly coming alive,
And upon it, hidden from view, life does thrive.

Vast areas of undulating plains,
Fine-tuned and tiny, miniscule grains,
Large batches of small stone getting underfoot,
Camels feet becoming a point of great moot.

No, life was not easy for the cameleer,
Not for the camel held so dear,
But they shared good company and love,
They fit together like hand and glove.

## THE DINGO

Close to camp for the night they did approach,
When Nak saw up front one of the many desert roach,
As the sun commenced its journey, to slowly disappear,
The night air incessantly cooled through progressive gear.

There was a dingo up ahead, a sure sign of trouble,
No matter mind of genius or even mind of rubble,
A dingo at dusk, waiting, looking, standing,
Was a recipe for disaster in the making.

And Nak felt he knew why the dingo was here,
Why the dingo was adamant to remain near,
The reason will be divulged to you soon,
With or without the comfort of light from sun or from moon.

"We have a dingo up front and we'll be camping shortly,"
"Will you shoot it?" asked Abdul rather curtly,
Nak replied: "Not just yet but on him maintain,
Good visual in order to counter his desire to gain."

"No need to upset the camel,
Too close to end of days travel,
Nose pegs to be removed,
Maybe after safety has been proved."

# AFGHAN

Shir asks: "What did you say?"
"I say keep your eyes open in case he decides to stay,
This damn dog called dingo looking for camel to play,
But deny him great sport I shall this day."

Shir says: "I know why,
Why he is here, why he is not shy,
My camel Slate is ready to give birth,
And I am prepared to receive great, ecstatic mirth."

"Slate has been grumbling a little now,
This past few minutes, that I do know,
Not long now I am sure of that,
Used to the signs, but now, no time to chat."

And not much further along,
They are ready for camp and for song,
"We camp here for the night,
Keep good visual, right and tight."

The procedure for setting camp was the same as before,
Though Shir made time to see Slate and to assure,
Unloaded her first and getting ready for birth,
Ready for young one to fall and to grow great girth.

Nak could see that the dingo had retreated a short distance,
But he did not retreat very far, ready for deliverance,
So Nak had to stroll over to Chocolate,
Get ready his rifle, he was not obstinate.

Prefer to let live the dingo,
Wishing him to be free and let go,
But camels came first before this creature,
Whose desire was for blood, it was in his nature.

He untied and prepared rifle for firing,
Feeling it a choir, this killing quite tiring,
The string of camels had all been seated,
He set the sights of weapon as was needed.

But waste the meat of dingo he would not,
Try all he could to wound and not allow to rot,
To kill according to law, for the good of all,
To not waste a bullet, or meat, forced to feel abysmal.

Bringing the rifle into his shoulder,
Looking out to front, through brush and past boulder,
Honestly too far even for Nak to shoot,
A missed target meant nothing to loot.

Nak did not wish to kill for the sake of killing,
Did not find it at all thrilling,
Didn't wish the dingo to crawl away and die in great pain,
But calf was under way, unto world of desert plain.

The other two men stood by their camel,
Abdul pleased their familiarity had grown during travel,
Slate rather slow to react to orders given,
Men busy unloading packs, skilful and driven.

# AFGHAN

No real telling how long before delivery,
But seemingly soon, be rid of the drudgery,
For even camels suffered the pains of labour, did stress,
Walking Slate may aid in the matter, avoid a stressful mess.

Nak aimed the rifle as best he was able,
The dingo standing front on, on all fours, stable,
But Nak missed his target completely,
Hardly jarring the dingo, it moving rather discreetly.

The animal then stopped and turned to stare,
A loud noise only, what did he care,
He'd barely moved, even to side, when shot was fired,
As the bullet whipped through the air, to vacuum retired.

Shir laughed and stirred a few camels, their glanced lent,
His laugh more disturbing than bullet just spent,
"Good shot, Nak," was what he did say,
"Concentrate next time you should, maybe another day."

"Lay upon target of flesh and bone,
Not stir him slightly as though throwing a stone."
Nak replied: "If you bend over, Shir, I shall not miss,"
And turned again to the dingo, "Watch this."

He reloaded and squeezed more gently this time, good site picture,
Breathed in and out, good comfort, good posture,
Fired his shot and the dingo he did hit,
Now sprawled on the ground, and Nak did spit.

A carcass wasted, no good to them now,
To the dark of the forever night the dingo did bow,
Now raw pickings for the creatures that do seek,
An easy meal to be had, slim pickings for the meek.

## THE BIRTHING

Not long after fireplace set,
Slate gave birth, new calf was met,
Of similar colour to mother,
Nothing out of ordinary than other.

The calf sought out the udder, no need to mention,
Good size and good son to mother interaction,
Good nourishment, great gift, an attraction,
Young calf with good sucking action.

"Good looking calf," said Nak, "he looks great,
You need to get a bag ready, prepare ride for Slate,
She can also carry the kitchen, with blessing,
A lighter load with rations diminishing."

"Take up the rear and follow from behind,
Not distract the others of duty and mind,
I shall go seek some more fodder to stow,
Abdul with me, please, to task, do follow."

Abdul pondered the request of company to keep,
Wondered on Nak's need to speak,
Nak was awaiting to divulge news in good turn,
Something to listen to, something to learn.

Abdul complied to the request, the bid, the need,
He could see it ahead, conversation a budding seed,
Leaving Shir with camel in newfound fame,
To return later to circle and talk around near fire and flame.

And of the calf we must briefly accost,
For they are heathen to look after but a blessing, no cost,
Much good rearing before working track can they take,
For their place on earth as movers, for living to make.

And currently to spare the anguish of walk ahead,
Calf would be bundled and bound instead,
Wrapped in bag and onto mother's back,
Along with cargo, added to stack.

During the trudge across desert plains and mound,
Slate would look over shoulder, joy bestowed and found,
Young calf blinking adorably at mum,
All content, all love, clear to see, an insurmountable sum.

Slate would be content to continue the move,
A part of the string, moving great trove,
Her body churning to make milk for her young,
Seven pints of milk from bladder to mouth and over tongue.

Until back in Marree would the unnamed calf be carried,
Until three years old, too young to be married,
To string with heavy load, not for long or short haul,
Much hard work in future but currently none at all.

# AFGHAN

After weaning it would be able to accompany its mother,
But no loaded store to kill and to smother,
A separate string attached to the caravan,
A nose peg worn as any other, it was not ban.

But this was not necessity, not entirely required,
Only if Slate needed would calf join as though wired,
It was capable of keeping up with the string, all would agree,
But preference would be for calf to remain in Marree.

From three years the calf would meet with work,
No time to be lazy, no time to shirk,
At eight years it would be mature,
Entirely and appropriately of good stature.

Nak and Abdul took a few steps more,
Before stopping in front of pantry, a store,
Spinifex available, easy picking,
Tussock grass easily cut like whittling.

Much Mulga around,
Grey foliage abound,
Seeds and pod,
A meal for which to nod.

Weeping mulga bush with silvery leaves, a good feed,
Saltbush from salty soil, good fodder suiting their need,
Covered in a white powder, blue-grey leaves do tease,
Sturts Desert Pea a favourite to see and appease.

Camels happy to eat whole bush and root,
Pulling from ground and shaking free the soil to loot,
Seeds dormant during dry times, little moisture,
Hairy grey-green stems, easy to eat, no torture.

It was all free, as free as can be,
As far as any man can see,
Filling hungry camels with much glee,
Cameleers could do nought but agree.

A camel would grab a branch in its jaw,
Not in teeth, pull down, stripping to gnaw,
Regurgitate, chew and chew,
Grinding all down until mellow like stew.

"You've been working hard," of Abdul, Nak did praise,
"How do you find it here, where camels for free do graze?
How do you like this Birdsville Track?
Few towns, few settlements, few homesteads, few shack."

"Much like the rest of the country I have seen,
Already growing dull but I am still eager and keen,
The scenery is beautiful and night skies are a gift,
Something to look forward to, to one's spirit it does lift."

"Ah, yes," agreed Nak, "Not much change about,
No gauntlet. No maze, no strict route to lay out,
But like you say it fills you up with something special,
Gives you purpose, feels gratifyingly simple; not social."

# AFGHAN

"For the nights do similar for me, it does lure,
Lifts my precious soul to heaven, no restriction, no mure,
Splendid feelings of solitude and private thought,
To contemplate the meaning of life, an understanding sought."

"But you still have much to see and experience,
Possibly rainy season to bring a little flood and grievance,
Flooded plain in some areas, for miles and miles around,
Nowhere dry, not a piece of dry ground to be found."

Abdul askes: "You have experienced this all?"
"All, around four years that have to me come to fall."
"And yet you have not made your fortune to date."
Nak looks Abdul in the eye, "One day: one day, it is not too late."

Nak educated: "It favours a man to keep many friends."
"Friends like Jehangir who mitigates, to new arrivals he tends?"
"Yes," said Nak, "friends to aid you always, in many ways,
We aid each other, many times over the years, across many days."

A compliment Abdul then did make,
"You have made much from nothing: much risk you did take."
Nak rpelied: "We have suffered risk and much, much more,
A reminder to me and Shir, a reminder of gore."

Abdul pressed on: "You do not speak of war?"
"No, no, I do not, but something more,
Of a man named Muschky, a good friend to adore,
I recall his death as though scribed, as though lore."

"He was shot dead, his head hit by a bullet,
Whilst doing a delivery, running goods as though through gauntlet,
Too close to a town we had travelled,
And we paid for it, most expensively, our empathy levelled."

"Little pity can I feel for most,
I feel more for Muschky even if a ghost,
I am not easily startled or made distrait by nature's mess,
Too much bad fortune, too much anguish, too much stress."

"Listen to me, Abdul, listen well,
Too few to be trusted here, no matter how you gel,
If no Koran they carry,
Then do not tarry."

"It is why we keep clear of the worn track,
Not just to appease the camel, upon softer sand, their knack,
But to remain aloof and away from the racism,
Save us from falling into cataclysm."

They moved over to where Slate was mothering,
Placed the harvest food before her, patient and waiting,
And Shir arrived at their side, no lag,
Having finished making, for calf, his travel bag.

Nak said: "The rifle I carry is not just for dire need,
It is also for self defence against growing, racist creed,
I have never yet needed to use it for much,
And never yet for defence, against maliciousness and such."

# AFGHAN

"When I look at the rifle I can see Muschky clearly,
Wishing to be a businessman, his heart set dearly,
Wished to work via contract with miners,
Supplying hotels and bars, to appease their diners."

"He wished to blend with the country about,
Not be lazy, to never be the lout,
To help this country in growth the best he could,
Was ambitious and keen, and tell a lie he never would."

"Never a sore word to say about anyone,
A heart made of pure love, not stone,
But last year was the undoing of it all,
His end met due to this racist gall."

"It was upon this very track,
We were near Mulka and checking some tack,
For a load had become a little loose,
And he wished to get camel's discomfort from noose."

"He then dropped dead, shot in the head,
Came out of nowhere, our hearts instantly filled with dread,
Possibly meant to scare, it came, a mighty thwack,
But it ricochet off some supplies on a camel's back."

"Maybe murder, maybe a mistake,
But little action could we take,
They rode away extremely fast,
Several people on horseback, we were simply aghast."

Nak asked, after a few seconds more,
"Why tell me this now, when past Mulka's door?
You could have told me of this before,
Instead of holding it within mind, in store."

Nak explained: "I've been fighting my soul since,
My feelings shrivelled, ground, turned into mince,
Killing the dingo reminded me so much,
Of Muschky and his kind heart, seemingly always in touch."

"I know I have proved to be reliable with weapon,
But the evil of killing has been a lesson,
Ever since Char Asiab and war,
My feelings have changed as though, from me, tore."

Nak a little astounded,
Shocked; grounded,
"You were at Char Asiab, just over four years before,
And then came here, hoping to never see more."

Nak continued: "Every day I experience fear, and I tire,
Of what the colonists may call my betrayal to Empire,
You, Abdul, fought for the British and have little to hide,
I tend to look over my back all day during my long ride."

"My ride to acceptance,
My ride from grievance,
My ride to great friendship,
My ride to avoid the punisher's whip."

# AFGHAN

"You are now a good friend,
And with friendship our inner souls do mend,
You felt strongly about fighting for them,
And I am the opposite, of different branch but same stem."

"But my life is here, now and forever, for the greater,
I shall never return home to be placed within fetter,
I wish to grow old and knowledgeable,
Of able body and mind, in old age be financially stable."

"I cannot be caught and found out,
To be convicted by any means, always silent, never to tout,
These people here will never listen to me,
Understand I am innocent, should be set free."

Nak, with furrowed brow: "What are you trying to say?"
"With my feelings, every day I do prey,
I want you to carry the rifle for me,
Of course, to refuse, you are free."

Nak said: "No, I am sorry your feelings do grapple,
But I cannot take it as though from tree to take apple,
Yes, I fought with the British,
But only in order to fill my family's dish."

"Sure, there were other reasons too,
To be fair there are many to throw in the stew,
But my families needs always came first,
And if I lie, may I die here in the desert, die of thirst."

Nak said: "I hold this not against you, I say,
But I appeal to your greater understanding, and may,
May you see it from my perspective,
For, from me, the outlook is only the negative."

"It would be easier for you to plead innocent,
If before court of law you are made present,
A greater scrutiny of my past,
Could see my days on earth made my last."

"But, I am aghast,
I have offended you to the last,
Just please understand my predicament here,
Of my past and the ashes I carry from last year."

Shir then spoke: "You should know everything,
I shall open to you and hide nothing,
You are the only one can carry the rifle,
With all these words we do not trifle."

"Nak is a wanted man and so am I,
It is nothing that I can really deny,
I am wanted, dead or alive,
For against the British I did strive."

"I should not tell you this but I shall,
It may hit you on head, like mallet to ball in pall-mall,
I am wanted as a spy by the British,
And for killing one, a mission I did wish."

# AFGHAN

"Only Nak and Muschky knew this before today,
And now you, and I hope that with you only it does stay,
We can both be easily sentenced, and heavily, put to death,
Death and no glory, no sanctification, to ground beneath."

"And I hear that question, set behind your eye,
The one that lingers but does not pry,
And the answer is no, do you, of me, hear?
You do not deserve judge and jury, before them to appear."

"But it is simply your ability to go against conviction,
To be announced innocent is an easy prediction,
If those that killed Muschky appear again,
Steady hand I fear I cannot maintain."

"A seconds delay in pulling the trigger,
Will see our misery grow all the bigger,
They will get away with another killing,
And we shall have to quit, give up this grinding."

"This is all upsetting to speak,
Our feelings are mixed and never seem to peak,
But I say to you now of my regret,
My poor feelings for British spy I killed, after we met."

"For without my prior, murderous killing,
I could easily do for what may be bidding,
Help defend Muschky's good memory,
To give closure to this entire story."

"I would happily take up rifle against these non-believers,
Defend against these devils, not grievers,
For they have not an ounce of pity for any living thing,
They do not care for anything breathing."

Abdul reflected on all that was spoken,
His heart torn, as though broken,
"Your secrets are safe with me, you need to know,
But I won't carry your rifle, on my camel never to stow."

Nak said after reflection, a second's thought:
"That's fair: you've heard the truth, we both have taught,
And I think soon we have to conclude with day,
Finish with prayer and share a meal if we may."

And all three have learnt a fair bit,
Of commitment: characteristic; being woven, being nit,
And before each closed his eyes for the night,
Each considered the company they had, and in it the great delight.

## THE THIRD DREAM OF CONSEQUENCE

The Punjab Infantry continued their advance,
Upon defensive position, battle at a glance,
Abdul having prepared his weapon once more,
Looking for a target, for life to take, a notch to score.

Dust flew up here and there,
Nothing but from enemy the evil stare,
And then from destiny of horror within dream,
He is snatched from it by voice, fluid as though from stream.

"Abdul, it is time to wake,"
Said Nak, for early day he wished to make,
"No time for sleep, prepare for the day,
Time to prepare, to be on our way."

Nak and Shir appeared to be happier than normally gifted,
A great weight from shoulder having been lifted,
But they saw reflection and uneasiness there,
Abdul's dreaming, his glancing off to distance in stare.

But all in all the truth had been revealed,
No longer was guilt of any description to be sealed,
And yet Abdul did seem off put by something unclear,
Something in his heart, something he did not hold dear.

Regardless of this predicament,
The homestead was a destiny set in cement,
Many hours and days remained to be cleared,
Many more miles for camels to be seared.

Abduls reflections of mind continued unabated,
Mostly for the worst they had been rated,
His dreams continued each night, ending never near,
And he felt he knew why but it wasn't entirely clear.

Feeling faintness was experienced on occasion,
As though his mind suffered a lesion,
And with the reflections of his mind,
Each day fell faster, the miles piling behind.

Time passed quickly, never regressed,
To the issue of delivery on time always stressed,
The second last night before homestead falling almost into sight,
The sun saying its farewell, praising its goodnight.

The camel string pulled up late as was normal,
Time for good rest before another day could fall,
Wide orange expanse on horizon, nice and tight,
A band of beauty, supposedly a sailors' delight.

Cicadas claimed the night for their own,
Their song joining that of the desert as though sewn,
Many voices of the night coming together as one,
Always together and never alone.

# AFGHAN

This was nature at its most splendid best,
Always at work and never at rest,
Cicadas song, male calling to mate,
A call to be heard, female attending as though fish to bait.

Their song was majestic, a repeated vibration,
Helping men sleep, after being filled with elation,
Nothing like life by a campfire at night,
To fold away worries and gift that feeling of delight.

To sleep that soundless sleep at night,
To wake in the morning feeling alright,
But the song needs to get gotten used to at first,
Like the suckling of a baby from mother, ecstasy burst.

A calming effect which is hard to explain,
Though from it good feelings we all can gain,
Though Abdul mused once more to be of a different mould,
Something having come over him, something clearly untold.

## HOMESTEAD, COME FARMER, NEAR

It was almost time, the time almost done,
The time of delivery and coin to be won,
Before saddling up again for return journey,
Goods from homestead to port, their conviction sturdy.

Little by little the world around was divulged,
Abdul taking it all in, names of places, a hidden map, it bulged,
The more he saw, the more was shared, and onwards drive,
And coming to last night before homestead they did arrive.

It was important for Abdul to know the land,
The whereabouts of settlement, homesteads and,
A police station, in future, its existence along the track,
Compared to a meal, not even a snack.

A police station was to be built near Diamantina to the north,
Just 15 miles shy of Queensland border for what is was worth,
A line marked on the map, not on land,
Hard to know in which state you did actually stand.

Diamantina Police Station most assuredly to arrive,
This year in fact, and little from it could you derive,
It would house three officers of the law,
The pitiful job and lives clinging as though to straw.

# AFGHAN

The police here would support the wider community,
A town on the grow, a much given opportunity,
Employed to enshrine the rules of society,
Ensure taxes were paid, not to be taken likely, a novelty.

Strict rules here, nothing left to slide,
Selling of unlawful alcohol would not be abide,
To become a sticking mess and sorrowful life,
The officers here married and single, possibly bringing wife.

Nak said: "The police station will require occasional supply,
With them a contract on which to possibly rely."
Shir added: "A reasonable job we can try and secure,
Maybe an opportunity to expand business for sure."

Abdul asked: "What will you do to contract mend?"
Nak replied: "I shall consider a friend of a friend,
I know a man in Marree that may be able to sway,
Voice good word and bring business our way."

"Fulfil Muschky's dream, one day we will,
Secure our futures, jobs similar to this will fit the bill,
Not much rest do we desire between jobs, we are men,
Rest can come later when we are with many strings, and then."

"I just pray that Ahmad Mohammed has something,
A job for us on return to Marree or we have nothing,
He is very gifted in many ways,
Well guided of mind, much conviction, strong stays."

"Who is he?" Abdul does ask,
Says Nak: "A man, for Faiz Mahomet he does work at many task,
And with small coin provided from my pledge,
He gifts us information and a little knowledge."

"He also has a weak spot and spends this on a prostitute,
Soft as melon in her company his mouth does shoot,
Divulges much more information, you would be aghast,
She provides this to us for errands of the past."

Abdul said: "The power of a woman,
Can never be underestimated: no confusion,
No doubt either do I have for their courage,
I believe it with all the sincerity I can manage."

Nak: "And Shir can attest to that, can you not?"
"I can, and do, so we all agree, here on this spot."
"Ha,ah!," voiced Nak, pointing a finger, "I see in your eyes,
You'd forgotten about her, your wife; tell me no lies."

"You care more for that camel, Slate and her calf,
Than any wife white man calls his other half,
Your camel is your real wife,
And will be for life."

Shir: "To think I care more for a camel instead,
Means that of me you clearly have misread,
I am devoted to Slate… I mean Arika ever more,
So… stop teasing me, before, before…"

# AFGHAN

"Before what?" jokes Nak, "That sound like rot,
Come, we are friends here, are we not?"
Abdul was laughing with Nak trying to smile wide,
Shir seemed to be happy to accompany on this ride.

"It was the delivery of the calf, being on my mind,
I grow tired of the hard, extra work, to you I wish to remind,
Hard work for me alone to carry out,
And never complain do I, never do I give a painful shout."

"Work!" continued Nak, "is not feeding a calf,
There is harder work for you in taking a bath."
"I'll have you know," said Shir quite seriously,
"I had a bath before married: twelve months early."

## NEAR THE QUEENSLAND BORDER

All three men woke just prior to the crack of dawn,
No time to reflect on lost sleep, no time to mourn,
Ablutions, prayer, breakfast, and pack and gather,
After which already covered in sweaty lather.

Though this morning was provided a little more time,
For homestead was not far, conversation to mime,
Broken English would need to be employed,
Sometimes hard to gather meaning, slang to avoid.

Meanwhile, amidst their thoughts during packing,
Shir was busy with Slate and calf, calf napping,
Nak busy with the camp and other chores,
Abdul gathering stray camels out-of-doors.

Abdul contemplated, as he walked,
That the rifle he should carry, forever on mind it stalked,
But he did not wish to carry it, not anywhere near,
It was hard to understand why, and he considered it could be fear.

Abdul heard a bell not too far ahead,
Silhouettes of camels easily read,
Eating the spinifex and anything else found,
If they could they'd eat it right to the ground.

# AFGHAN

On occasion the camels were hard to spot,
Blend into the surrounds more readily than not,
But cameleers were used to searching them out,
Whether by sound of bell or by simply looking about.

Abdul saw then that one of the camels was blowing its bladder,
Excitement building within it, and not to slander,
Looks unappealing, but to another camel,
Ready for mating, quite healthy and natural.

Of the mating ritual, another creature does not mimic,
Cameleers used to camel smells, even the most prolific,
And the sight of soft palate hanging from mouth, seemingly stout,
Repugnant sacks, and foot long foam, hanging thereabout.

The male will then deposit upon bark, and the like, a great stink,
Big slatherings of black patches, of tar-like-ink,
Rubbing against bark and anything else which vision does fall,
Anything  to brush against, anything at all.

When Abdul arrived back after his achieved recovery,
He divulged to Nak of his discovery,
Told him it may be Joy, of the blowing bladder,
Not sure of its name but feeling all the gladder.

Nak advised: "Yes, that one is called Joy, your right,
When at the homestead we shall keep him out of sight,
They will not appreciate the smell,
And our relationship needs to further gel."

"I am trying hard for next  years contract, too,
Much work for us, much work for us to do,
The man's name is Alfred, seemingly, though unlikely lazy,
His wife's name sounds quite simply crazy."

Abdul responded: "A strange name indeed,
And a new name she is in much need."
"No, Abdul, that is not it, not her name,
I was advised her name is Marge, crazy but tame."

"We must refer to them as Mr and Mrs Stapleton,
I'm told that both are walking sticks, mere skeleton,
Hard times in the bush, they are as thin as thin can be,
Unlike in the city where food does, to all, agree."

"I see you have all the camels gathered,
Good work, Abdul, now time to get them tethered."
Abdul explained without need: "They followed Chocolate,
As though leading to great waters they did come, first rate."

Nak said further: "Maybe they know, maybe they smell,
That tomorrow at homestead they shall water well,
But seeing them gathered so easily gives pleasure,
Maybe we are in time for good fortune and in good measure."

## OF FARMER AND WIFE

The homestead came into view, quite picturesque,
Beauty bound, a home, an office without front desk,
A small business to sprout, to serve the couple's need,
Time to grow, time to fill wont, desire, inner greed.

For all men and women alike toiled through life,
Quest for money and avoid anything rife,
Future retirement, old age always on mind,
But to get there most people, through life do grind.

There was a wooden house here,
A storage shed beside it did appear,
Another for the shearing of sheep,
Another in which for wool to keep.

A small windmill drew water from ground,
Ample quality and quantity had been found,
Not far sat a dry creek bed,
With water in wet season to be wed.

Slightly set upon higher ground,
More so than what around them did surround,
It was a place to call home, but not so happily,
Not a place to live forever, for most just temporarily.

Mulga grew in many places upon this 'farm',
Culled back by the eucalyptus, causing no harm,
Large Australian trees found nation-wide,
Eucalyptus the camels could not abide.

Of all the things in the bush to eat,
Eucalyptus, to camels' stomach, would unlikely meet,
It is untrue to say that they do not eat these,
More so that they do not, at all, to their needs appease.

Standing before the door to house rubbing his hands,
Hand in the dirt before he then stands,
Abdul can see the farmer [pastoralist] getting ready for meeting,
To shake hands in this, their formal way of greeting.

A feeling of surprise by what happened next could not be denied,
The shaking of hands was never met, was not to meeting applied,
But a nod of the head was exchanged instead, no grace,
This was the most solemn hello to be found upon this place.

Nak greeted Alfred as the man stood there in trousers, unclean,
Holes in shirt aplenty could be seen,
Worn fabric, stains and blemishes galore,
Poor man in tatters, conclusion drawn from what he wore.

Alfred removed his hat most temporarily away,
Not for good manners but to wipe sweat aside this hot day,
He returned it fast before communication did commence,
Nak wishing to open in order to establish good trade for pence.

# AFGHAN

---

*"So,"* said Nak, *"wool ready, where this token?"*
Alfred understood that broken English was to be spoken,
"You see, over there beside the house, you look,
You take and put on camel, after unload, then took."

Nak asked: *"Where unload; what you mean?"*
"Oh, look; I wish to work fast, get done, I am keen...
Over there, in the shed,"
Alfred then indicated with a move of his head.

Nak heard the frustration, the words in his head toiled,
Didn't wish to unload his stores upon ground to be soiled,
Thought he understood, finally, he was to unload upon floor,
The floor of the shed on which to place his stock, his store.

Nak was initially concerned for the rainy season,
He had forecast good care for the goods for this reason,
Was it possible that Alfred would move them again later,
Was it that the shed's ground was safe from water.

*"Ah, okay. You lucky,"* said Nak, *"No vermin this place."*
"No what?" asked Alfred with a curious look upon his face,
*"No rat; you no rat here in shed."*
"Ah; yes, plenty rat, but we cat, the shed is his bed."

"Rats are right across this damn country, all over they appear.
What do you think; we don't have rats up here?"
Alfred was forgetting himself, felt this might take all night,
Nak tried to confirm: *"Unload on ground, yes; is this right?"*

---

"No!" replied Alfred in a huff. "off ground, up; away from wet."
*"Okay, I work now,"* said Nak and turned away, his duty to be met.
Nak turned to Shir and Abdul, explained it all,
Of the work to be conducted, no time to stall.

Good quality of wool, good product to be giving,
If you could master hard work and hard living,
Fight against the the bouts of 'farmers' depression,
And stress a future of grand life, even if an illusion.

Two alternatives and from these a choice to make,
Bullock teams or camel strings, which road to take,
Bullock teams were mastered by white folk,
Camel strings by Afghans, holding the invisible yoke.

Strings were preferred for speed and agility,
What a shame they were immigrants, despite ability,
Delays could not be risked by any degree,
And so camel strings were employed, despite lack of glee.

To Alfred the camel industry had expanded vigorously,
The need and desire for them was spreading contagiously,
And for Nak the longevity of work came at a price,
That you were willing to work hard and always play nice.

Be courteous and cool to customer,
Shrug off all poor sentiment and slander,
Swallow your pride and be humble,
Never, before a customer, be caught to grumble.

# AFGHAN

The homestead here was isolated,
Far from train station, to market, related,
Unconditional contact was here for the taking,
Stores dropped and picked up, good work in the making.

Nake looked to the camels, all in a line,
Several having fidget slightly, waiting to dine,
But more than this they needed water,
No need to punish them, no need to slaughter.

Chocolate was spied chewing on cud, hidden behind lip split,
Hidden behind thick lips covered in dust and ready to spit,
30lbs of pressure and half gallon of filth upon white man to spill,
A vision Nak saw in momentary dream state, a shrouded ill-will.

The unloading of camels was taken to fast,
Alfred having filled water trough, from tower, to last,
Each camel to water and water in stomach to swell,
To take all he could, lesson of water gluttony, learnt well.

The Afghan men continued to work,
When Shir saw the wife, on lips a light smirk,
Approach a package bound in red cloth, well wrapped,
Like a map, big X on paper, well mapped.

She turned to see her only child of three quite safe from camel,
Safely hitched with rope, to home, not underfoot to be trample,
Shir saw Nak speaking with farmer, unaware,
Shir continued to watch with unsavoury flare.

Marge, clearly stupid and plain,
Took the parcel to unwrap for all to see, insane,
Risking all for something, nothing at all,
A hunk of salted pork, soon to be slivers onto frying pan to fall.

This woman, half-witted and hellish,
Openly rude and condemningly selfish,
Pig meat, from pig, having rolled in its faeces and muck,
Physically and spiritually unclean, for Shir the horror struck.

The Koran forbid the eating of pig,
The mullah prohibited its transport with any string or rig,
Even transporting tin cans with no label was fury tempting,
Was not permitted, was shunned, was extremely offending.

"Nak; Nak!" shouted Shir, with fluster and need, with great desire,
Terror in his eyes wrought with horror, attention he did acquire,
"What is it!" blurted Nak, suddenly concerned for friend,
For much empathy did he have for familiar, to the very end.

"There, the woman," pointed Shir, eyes scourging upon pig,
Finger pointing, "We've been transporting bacon, a piece so big."
Nak stomped over to Alfred with grimace upon mouth,
Scarred lips twisted in fashion, "*What this?*" empathy gone south.

Alfred saw the importance of the matter,
But reliable transportation he did not wish to shatter,
Putting hands up in denial and trying to defend,
His mind working hard as ever, to fix this issue, to mend.

# AFGHAN

"Wait!" said Alfred as he stepped back and blurted,
"Sorry; me sorry," and by now all had been alerted,
"*You damn man*," cursed Nak. "*You very bad.*"
"*You are crazy, so crazy, you is... very mad.*"

He was now steeped in perspiring anger,
His only way out was for he to discipline her,
Alfred stepped up over towards his wife,
And delivered a smack to face, his hardest in life.

The sound clapped out for all to hear,
She had been administered, it was plain and clear,
The bacon falling to the dry and cracking ground,
Alfred jumped up and down on the meat, and it did astound.

The woman burst out sobbing,
To red mark on face so deep did commence rubbing,
Alfred yelled: "I need this sale to go ahead without a hitch,
You stupid, stupid, stupid bitch."

Alfed peered over at the Muslim men three,
Hoping for his transport of goods as was agree,
Said Alfred: "My wife is so ridiculously stupid; I did not know,"
"It is finished now, The meat is ruined and into desert I throw"

But this was not enough for Nak today,
Even seeing the wife upon ground where she lay,
"*No*," said Nak, sorry for what had been done.
"*No more work. You do wool, no us, do it... alone.*"

"No, wait," pleaded Alfred, forgetful to whom he was speaking,
His broken English was overwhelmingly leaking,
"I didn't know about the bacon, I swear it, from me to thee.
If I'd known I would have stopped it in Marree."

Alfred could see the contract falling from grasp,
Needed to gather his wits, use any ploy to grip, to rasp,
Alfred needed money from trade for future to nurse,
More than Nak needed coin or banknote in purse.

Alfred calmed a little then: "I pay more, little extra for you,
New contract, no string, we do business, much to do,
I pay for five more days on road, can we upon this agree,
And you get paid at post office in Marree."

Alfred had one more piece of leverage to employ,
"You give note to John Arthur O'Brien, then no more annoy,
You give post office and he pay much; you understand?
We together good commerce, you, me, and this land."

Nak was slow to respond but nod his head he did,
Having looked at the others they were waiting to see his bid,
But Nak had nothing he wished to pry from this man,
His only real wish was to deliver goods, as was his plan.

Alfred said: "No more bacon, come sunshine or rain,
Never any more; all finished; never see again."
"*Okay*," said Nak. "*We do... job, for... relationship and for you.
We water camel, load wool; we go Marree, this thing, we do.*"

# AFGHAN

"Oh, thank you, thank you," said Alfred so happy,
His anxiousness now replaced by contentment real snappy,
"Ask for more money," said Shir in his native tongue,
"Take from him what means the most, for all he has flung."

"No," said Nak. "I won't become one of them, never at all,
*We do job, is okay*, said Nak. "*Bacon no more, in lap to fall.*"
"Yes, yes; thank you," said Alfred and with Nak shook his hand,
Not much can be said, really, for Alfred's final stand.

And so with sudden forgetfulness and with great ease,
Camels were lowered upon their knees,
Stores unloaded, watering still to be done, in this yard well fenced,
Loading of wool then pursued before return journey commenced.

## THE BILLABONG

It was late of day when reloading had been complete,
Their parting with white folk politely discrete,
The farmer optimistic and pressuring,
The wife, confused and befuddled, meandering.

The cameleers were respectful and courteous,
Though these outwards feelings were tirelessly laborious,
The camels, seemingly nocturnally, oblivious,
Not caring for either, but their nucleus.

Nak did mean to attend a billabong nearby,
One such passed, not far, where shade did lie,
A place to further water the camels, to quench,
To tighten up their resilience as though with wrench.

With bags of wool loaded and ready for market,
A scratch on calendar their date, their target,
Get goods to station on time and save,
The extra day's wage that promissory note gave.

It did appear as all was travelling well,
Though boring their days, their confidence swell,
Work had now been established and confirmed,
Their position and standing with Alfred well termed.

# AFGHAN

The water hole did not take long to reach,
Very small but solemn, solitude to teach,
Unpack the camels one more time this day,
Before much later heads lowered upon ground to lay.

But rituals and prayer were the usual items of respect,
Their religion never did fade, was never prone to neglect,
And watering of camels did continue for awhile,
Waterlilies and fronds, both visions, opposite to desert most vile.

The camels stood politely upon the edge of small pool,
Unlike oxen that bath in drinking water like fool,
Afghan men also heeding good sanitary rule,
No need to inhibit this sanctuary, its cleanliness, don't maul.

A water fowl was then seen amongst the slightly thicker scrub,
Not wishing to be the centre of attention, the nub,
And air bubbles in a few places within the shade of the few trees,
Did cry out in silence as though trying to tease.

You could not associate the farm of Alfred with billabong near,
A complete change to the homestead which to heart did tear,
A beastly, hurtful husband and pouting wife,
Too short is our time here on earth, too short is life.

The amount of water here was enough for their need,
Enough for them to continue on journey, to complete their deed,
Enough moisture here for the circle of life to drive,
Drive the combine of nature though it did not thrive.

Abdul went to fetch some wood for fire,
When lifting small log something did occur, rather dire,
He was stung savagely upon the little finger of left hand,
A deep red circle of fire around puncture, a band.

An unfortunate occurrence to be struck so swiftly in a flash,
By a scorpion of the bush having been disturbed it did lash,
Lash out with stinger as was its defensive nature,
A sting so brutal despite tiny stature.

Though a scorpion bite is not deadly in Australia,
This being widely accepted as idyllic, as though realia,
It was no fault of the scorpion so black and afraid,
Defending against intruder, upon his territory a raid.

The upturned wood disturbing the peace,
The tranquil solitude, the scorpions niche,
The fear bestowed upon it unfair,
As though looked in the eye by evil stare.

Abdul was so fast to withdraw his hand,
He failed to look for the assailant, the brand,
For to know the species by description may aid, provide,
Provide aid when advising the others, their knowledge a guide.

He cradled his left hand against his chest,
Raced back the short distance to campfire and nest,
His confusion and panic not helping at all,
Thoughts for his family at home, the first to call.

# AFGHAN

Abdul was strong and young,
His body able to deal with being stung,
It should be nothing for him to deal with grief,
But the pain of the wound made him grit his teeth.

The finger of his hand was already pulsing,
His thoughts now gone from family to pain engrossing,
This engrossing pain that should mean nothing to him,
But it was a fixture upon his mind, his frame, his figure trim.

"Shir! Nak!" yelled Abdul so loud,
Desert kick up behind his heels as though cloud,
Those of the campfire a little astounded,
Abdul yelling and usually quite rounded.

The silhouette of his two and only real friend,
Assured him and provided a temporary mend,
His sanity levelling and now restored to formal,
Though pain was quite evident, not deemed normal.

Nak had dropped his mug of tea and stood real fast,
Shir too, ready to aid to the last,
Bliss of the night stirred irregularly out of place,
Gone was any scene or picture of grace.

"Nak! Look; I've been bitten," Abdul explained,
He controlled his emotions, his sanity now reigned,
"Over there, by the wood, where the ground...
Look at my finger; the pain does pound."

Nak said: "Move closer to the fire, I can see better by the light."
Shir looked as closely as Nak: "It's not a snake bite."
"No?" said Abdul, not a question, wishing to optimistically agree,
"No," concurred Nak. "It's a scorpion sting, see."

Nak confirmed: " Look, one tiny puncture mark,
No single or double fang... of snake this does not loudly bark,
The redness is clear and no venom seeping from puncture,
Asked Abdul: "How do you know? Are you sure of this lecture?"

"I've seen bites before, Abdul," Nak explained,
"Plenty men have died by snake bite gained,
But you will not die, my friend so keen,
Besides, it is too late in the day for a snake to be seen."

Abdul complained: "But it hurts so much,
I cannot even, to wound, softly touch."
Nak said further: "The pain will go away,
Though meanwhile it will, with you stay."

Nak continued: "I know the basic treatment to the letter,
Maybe tomorrow you will feel a lot better,
Though other than that there is not much we can do,
Other than give you rest, and ensuring rest is up to you."

"Wash delicately in cool water as best you might,
Allow exposure to cold air this very night,
That is the best and only strategy I know: come sit by the fire,
You should be fine by tomorrow, early to bed, to retire."

## AMPUTATION

They sat around the fire and looked one another in the eye,
Two thankful and confident that Abdul would by no means die,
Abdul had faced death many times in his short life,
In some people religion did aid, in others pain of death was rife.

So what is the meaning, whether true or not, this internal myth,
One may say that God will greet them when cold and stiff,
That long life be had in heaven amidst peace and God's thrall,
Why still cling to life, shrug off death, and cry that inner waterfall.

Each and everyone is not built the same,
Some panic and thrash, some remain tame,
Others lose all sanity, no grasp on situation's gravity,
But others offer cheery smile to comfort those living in perplexity.

No need to be baffled though by life or by death,
We are each born, we blink, we die with last breath,
Though it is always better to die with grace,
Rather than greet one's last day in disgrace.

The fire of the camp was by now well lit,
Nothing left of the day but to talk and to sit,
But the pain of Abdul's finger was on his mind,
Was attacking his sanity, it began to grind.

Abdul said: "It's getting late, it's almost dark,
The visions I see of my finger are indeed stark."
Asked Nak: "What can we do?
I think we discuss it no more, it is through."

Said Abdul from heart: "I need to amputate it now,"
Nak looked from Abdul to Shir, empathy did not show,
Nak reprimanded then with: "Are you mad?"
But Shir defended Abdul: "No, a gift of mercy should be had."

Abdul pleaded of Nak: "This thing must be done, for me,
With you from bottom of heart I do plea,
My arm has already starting to blossom red,
The poison is flowing, this is easily read."

Nak did lecture: "What is amputation of finger going to achieve,
I see in your eye, I know you do grieve,
But the poison is pain, in your arm, not your finger,
It will dissipate, it will go, it will not linger."

Abdul said: "The finger is my source of pain,
Please take it off, now, I do ask you again."
Nak: "The source of your pain is your arm,
The poison in finger is doing you no harm."

Abdul: "It will take away the source of the pain, I say,
And it is my finger, my decision to make if I may,
Trust me Nak, it will not affect my efforts, nor my work
Missing a little finger will not see me, responsibilities shirk."

# AFGHAN

Nak said bluntly: "And your arm, the poison...
Amputate that, me, take an arm from person?"
"I hope not, Nak, but if it must be done,
Allow this poison to fester and this blasted country has won."

Shir knew that a lost finger was better than worse,
And so from him his true feelings, not just to nurse,
"He's right," concurred Shir. "He should take off the digit,
Take no chances, secure a future, move fast, not fidget."

Shir continued: "I recall a man from Afghanistan village,
Whose sanity and mind was savagely pillage,
They took off his finger under similar circumstances,
There are in fact few differences."

"Yes," said Abdul. "I too have heard, sanity, no sense of bliss—."
Burst Nak: "Yes, yes, we have 'all heard' of this,
That story is old, and has been told many times over,
Much forgotten in translation, from one mouth to another."

Nak continued: "You cannot believe in fables,
A story that float the breeze, as though it ambles."
Pleaded Abdul with sincerity, "Look at me,
Look into my eyes, what do you see?"

Nak did as was asked and felt the hurt within,
Recalled how he felt, scarred mouth, unable to grin,
A torment of life since Char Asiab which did adhere,
To be with him now and forever, from year to year.

"Okay," said Nak. "I'm the *jemadar*, my responsibility.
But it is a great shame, a great pity."
Said Abdul: "Thank you, Nak, thank you,
I believe it is the best thing to do."

Shears... clippers for the cutting of hair,
Employed for many reasons and in good repair,
Cast in rust stains but oiled well,
Miniature guillotine about to leash hell.

Nak said: "These will do," as he held up the sheers,
And he received voiceless nods of head from peers,
"It'll work as good as a knife... for sure,
I shall use them speedily, avoiding built pressure."

"I'll not use them as I would normally,
I need to apply sharp force, one cut, strategically,
"Abdul," explained Nak. "I'll simply hold the sharp edge,
Hold it over, to hilt of finger, at palm's ledge."

Of reassurance Abdul did give: "It's okay, Nak, of this I am sure,
Of the pain I honestly cannot take much more,
Of this dilemma I actually never considered, never saw,
Of all the things in life, this was never of mind, never in store."

Nak said: "Place your finger here, upon this rock,
Other fingers held back, under palm do lock,
I will place the edge of shears just here,
Before hitting on back of blade, the finger to shear."

# AFGHAN

"It will hurt Abdul, more than I'll know, so hold steady."
Abdul: "It can't hurt me any more than I hurt already,
I can't take much more of this absurdist pain,
Let the rock fall, a single harsh hit, no tepid drops of rain."

Nak looked to Shir as he placed the blade over receiver,
Places the rock in own hand ready to deliver,
"Look away, Abdul, so you don't flinch,
Don't move a muscle, or we could be in a pinch."

"Are you ready Shir, with the bandage and cloth?
Are you ready, on command, to willingly doth?"
Said Shir: "Yes, ready and steady, right now, I am—."
And then Abdul said, "Me too, I am—" but it was a sham.

For Nak hit hard before Abdul had finished, delivering the gift,
Nak having delivered powerful hit after rock he did lift,
Momentum of rock coming down fast behind Shroud,
Token words to prepare, but given, followed by shriek so loud.

And in this Abdul was fortunate,
For the finger came away, not obstinate,
Did not hang from flesh or strip of skin,
It was clean and quick, Nak did inwardly grin.

And within a split second of the hit being made,
Abdul pulled hand back so fast, to chest it was bade,
But Shir interfered and pulled hand out for wound to patch,
To cover it with white cloth and bandage to match.

Within a few seconds more,
Abdul did open the door,
"The pain is horrible and bad,
But nowhere near what was sending me mad."

Abdul then looked to hand where finger was normally found,
And then he saw it there, upon the ground,
Nak picked it up and threw it away,
Amongst the spinifex, the land a disarray.

Nak said: "That's it, there's nothing left to do,
Now rest, for you until morning, nothing for you,
If the paralysis in the arm does not go away,
Rest you must gain for at least another day."

Said Abdul: "My arm may..."
May have to come off, I don't wish to sound grey."
Nak replied: "That's not grey, that is black,
But such expertise I do lack."

"If the arm is to be removed it is not for me to do,
Only a doctor can do this... this voodoo,
Heinous it is to do such a thing, even if no choice can be made,
If worse comes to worst we will try and gain aid."

"Our task is now to see you well,
And get camels to station with instructions to sell,
If you die upon journey then that is not for me to decide,
It is unfortunate and by no means a comfortable ride."

# AFGHAN

"Maybe we will be delayed by a few days or such,
But the delivery will be made, another trophy to touch,
There is always a train ready at Marree to depart,
Let's be optimistic, turn bad fortune to good, become it an art."

Shir asked: "Will Stapleton be settled with that?"
"Possibly not, but it's for a bad man and wife with brat,
Thou even he knows that you can't rule the weather,
As such: no matter what brand of animal does make the leather."

And unfortunate it was that Nak should say this,
For even a healthy heart can a beat miss,
Sunny days and clear nights are not guaranteed,
It is not something in which you can plead.

But Shir had something up his sleeve,
Something he held back, something he could not alone, leave,
"Listen, Abdul, I have something saved for future,
It may help you, digest it, it may nurture."

He pulled from his pocket a container, a small vile,
A glass bottle with dry herbs, or other: a trial,
"I had this thing stored with Slate,
This will aid your well-being, lift it from grate."

"It's an Aboriginal concoction, provided me by Arika,
A gift before leaving her side, I do miss her,
She advises to add a little water, take all if infection sets in,
I give it to you, so lift up that chin."

"Thank you, Shir, I know not what to say,
I am feeling great friendship now instead of feeling grey,
I shall try this medicine, try it right now,"
And so added water and drained it all, and coughed, "Wow."

AFGHAN

---

## THE FOURTH DREAM OF CONSEQUENCE

Abdul is ignoring the moaning of the dying as it grew,
And sees an enemy soldier, head appearing into view,
It bobs down and up again several times in a row,
The anxiety in the enemy can be seen to grow.

The enemy suddenly leaps from the small fortification,
Ready for evacuation, giving up on his pride and nation,
Abdul points his rifle at the enemies head,
Fires off a shot as trigger is manipulated and read.

The enemy's head turns at the same instant,
It is Nak, plain as day, a militant,
Abdul's bullet strikes him in the mouth, ending the task,
Nak is shot, the grimace on face, his eternal mask.

## THE STORM

The next day revealed much unpleasantness for all,
Particular for Abdul; the gathering of camels seemed to stall,
Normally much easier to gather but today one hour more,
Wider area of ground covered across desert, a longer tour.

It was in the mind of the camel, animals were able,
They knew what was coming, inward feelings unstable,
A storm was coming and would be upsetting to most,
A smell upon the wind, a warning strong with ambition to boast.

Abdul put the kitchen away,
None happy with the delay,
Nak and Shir had also been slow in retrieval,
Nak said: "Something has upset the camels, some evil."

Shir also: "And your arm, Abdul, better than when you woke?"
"I think that vile of medicine, is working, no need to joke,
Just this past hour alone has seen an improvement,
I feel much better, and my arm, much freer movement."

Nak: "It's all in the head,
It is easily read,
I have no faith in concoctions,
Only for Allah and his revelations."

# AFGHAN

Shir: "We all agree with that doctrine,
But with good faith and medicine...
Joining the two in union,
Racked layers around the core of onion."

"The more good we do the better off we are,
Whether from Koran, vile, onion or jar,
Remedies to improve one's health,
Just charge in and heal, no reason for stealth."

Nak applauded: "Maybe you are right,
Self help and remedies do keep a mind tight,
But so long as Abdul gets better I really am not concerned."
Shir returned: "And I believe in Arika, will not have her spurned."

Nak said: "Well, let us all agree on this one thing,
No matter the remedy or belief it has taken potency from sting,
Abdul is feeling better and together we are strong,
But with the camels there is something wrong."

Abdul smiled and turned, work to be found,
Proud of what he had accomplished with one hand bound,
In more pain than Shir and Abdul could ever realise,
But awkwardly unable to slow down: full of enterprise.

Nak said: "Just get the camels loaded, and  ready to move,
Once loaded it will be time for us all to get in the groove."
They all smiled at the sound of this tune,
When Abdul looked up, ghastly image, to temperament prune.

His expression did change and become rather solemn,
Knew now the reason for the camels, their problem,
The others saw his jaw drop and followed his gaze,
There before them was something to amaze.

Out upon the horizon and approaching them fast,
Was something more than mythical, and it was going to last,
From north to south and across the entire expanse of sky,
Something clear as day, something you could not deny.

A darkened mass of billowing red sand, fiercely mean,
A thick curtain so tall it was absurdly obscene,
Within all their courage had taken a dive,
They had but three minutes to react before it did arrive.

Sandstorms are not very frequent,
But bestowed much fear, much fear to be lent,
The storm approaching was the most ominous Nak had ever seen,
Currently silent but growing, so menacing and mean.

Dark cloud and sand pelleting around,
And then came the feeling, the vibrating ground,
Enormous bellowing surge of force of nature,
Seen now as mushrooming balls, an unstoppable structure.

A storm may last a few hours to several days,
Endeavouring to navigate through such was like walking a maze,
You can hardly open your eyes to see,
No knowing from whence you come and where you need to be.

# AFGHAN

Nak ordered: "Quickly, Shir, get the shelter from the saddle,
Put it up over there next to the mulga tree, away from camel,
Abdul, get the water and some biscuits from saddle of Slate,
We don't have much time; quickly now, before it's too late."

The men rushed to their assigned task,
Their actions the complete opposite of bask,
Shir saw to it that the calf was also untied,
No need to hobble, he would remain at mother's side.

Hobble! They had no time, with this could not be concerned,
The camels may wander off, no telling as events in time turned,
Nak had already unrolled and hastily erected the shelter,
Having performed well amidst the helter-skelter.

The shelter was set sturdily, ground level, low,
To avoid the worst of the storm as it did blow,
Avoid the storms menacing, overpowering thrust,
The billowing hate, its desire to deliver harmful lust.

Enough protection here to avoid sand though not flying debris,
Not enough room to sit and enjoy a mug of tea,
Not enough here to cook and chat away,
Only room to lay and to pray.

"Nak!" jolted Shir for the *jemadar's* attention,
"I did untie the calf from Slate, I thought I should mention."
"Again with you and that damn calf of yours,
Surprised I am you didn't bring it here, indoors."

With camels quickly forgotten and shelter briskly erected,
Quick and vast thought was spent on anything neglected,
And most important of all: "The Koran! We need it," Shir blurted,
Nak and Abdul now alerted.

Nak was the *jemadar*, knew where it was stored,
Strategy quick to form, the storm had to be ignored,
Without further ado he crawled from beneath their protection,
An attempt to now gain what was of mention.

For Nak this was the storm of all motherly storms that exist,
As though a blanket was cast upon the world, a mist,
But this mist was such a dark mass or sand blown red,
That it was hard to see, to blindness this lead.

If one cannot open his eyes to see around,
To see where moving, to view the ground,
If unable to negotiate any given track,
Then this is blindness, sense of sight Nak now did lack.

The sun was also blot out or sight and mind,
There was no solace in the world to find,
This was sheer bleakness on a tremendous scale,
Last straw to camel, to coffin last nail.

Nak relied upon common sense and thought,
Rational thinking and evaluation heavenly sought,
It was day and now it was night, you could not hear anyone shout,
The howling of wind and storm was so loud, all about.

# AFGHAN

No sense of direction,
No sight to mention,
No sound for clarity,
This storm a rarity.

Nak felt his way slowly and surely,
Memorising every shrub and stone, the morning still early,
Camels untied and near ready for loading,
Would be lined in a file, easy for finding.

He would move on hands and knees,
Feeling his way with relative ease,
Angle of approach set upon his mind,
Counting camels for Koran to find.

The camels, built for weather, were much better off,
Treating it as though kings and queens, acting the toff,
Closing their nostrils and breathing through slit,
Denying penetration of fine sand, any form of grit.

Hair within nose filtering what may penetrate,
Built in, natural, as good as any filtration or grate,
The camel's eyes were also fifty percent opaque,
Easier for them to negotiate safe track to take.

The severity of storm was obvious from onset,
The absolute worst Nak had ever met,
The stinging grains thrashing against flesh of face,
His mind scrawling map, and for Koran a race.

The noise had become deafening to say the least,
Camels were silent, laying in wait, a most resilient beast,
No sound for Nak to go by or vision to appease,
Death from becoming lost, fear to mind, it did tease.

He then fell upon a camel and felt around,
Remained on knees, camels also upon ground,
They were weathering out the storm,
And the temperature around was still very warm.

For the breeze was coming from the desert's heart,
Where heat was like furnace, from where storm did start,
Dry and humid, hot and dry, the storm so wide, so tall,
A devastating condition, the worst conditions of all.

Stacked against Nak, no favour,
Nothing around to savour,
But familiarity with camel string he did hold,
Knew where to find his Koran, felt inspired and bold.

The pressure upon his eyelids was beginning to build,
He had nothing to aid him, nothing to shield,
The pressure of quitting was present at large degree,
Continue he must, this was about 'team' not 'me'.

Suddenly, and with great relief,
He fell upon the place of Koran, a lifting of grief,
The great book soon secure, pushed inside clothing with finger,
No time now to stay and consider, no time to rest or to linger.

# AFGHAN

He remained on the ground, kept on crawling,
Making his way back, foot by foot, upon mind scrawling,
He pressed onwards picturing all in his mind,
Hoping way back to easily find.

He screamed at the top of his lungs for Shir and Abdul to hear,
Wondered whether or not they may be quite near,
Ferocity of the wind shredding his words into mince,
Even he, himself, could not hear himself, and he did wince.

Back under shelter Abdul did try to speak,
Now yelling to Shir, hoping his words, to Shir's ear, would leak,
He placed cup of hand over Shir's ear then tried again,
"Will Nak be okay?" expressing concern, he did not refrain.

Shir reached for Abdul's ear and yelled in reply,
"Nothing is wrong, on his ability you can rely,
There is nothing we can do as this storm continues to pound,
For if he is lost then he will never be found."

## DILEMMA AND DESPAIR

Upon Nak time was taking its toll, torment to shower,
He'd been in the storm for almost an hour,
The thrashing upon body was too much to take,
Try for some form of shelter he must make.

He fumbled on in the darkness, Koran now held in tight of hand,
Providing him with some feeling of peace, a resilience, a stand,
A stand against adversity, against this devastating storm,
Respite received, wriggling upon the ground like a worm.

Happy and content with Koran in grasp, medicinal, a nurse,
Prepared to accept the worst of the worse,
And then he thought of his friends in the dark that last,
They had no Koran, "Blast this storm; blast, blast, blast."

He remained upon the ground and then grain upon grain,
Grains of the storm pillared around, upon him a great stain,
Commencing to bury him partially, his human nakedness,
To become part of the landscape, undulated in darkness.

Buried alive! Would anyone find him?
Would his burial place be discovered, could death be so grim?
His body to be fodder for ants and for more,
What of Saki of the Ghantown, the one and only he did adore.

# AFGHAN

How he would miss her, for she was his choice,
He did so cherish her comfort and her soft voice,
No! He wouldn't allow this to happen,
Would not allow this lonesome death to shapen.

Even if he had to remain outside in the storm,
He couldn't freeze to death, it was too warm,
Time without food: his thoughts could, any hunger, smother,
A little lack of water; Meh, so a little he may suffer.

But what if the storm lasted longer?
How long could it last; was he, of storm, the stronger?
He would search out a large rock, procure safe hide,
Or even a camel, lay beside it, avoid the sand, this devilish tide.

Inside the shallow shelter created,
Nak's possible survival was on term to be rated,
Abdul and Shir were both concerned for their friend,
Though this misery of theirs they could not mend.

They had biscuits to eat,
Water for which lips to meet,
Each other to comfort despite lack of sound,
Unable to see well and huddled so close to ground.

An endless cycle of emotions raging within,
Thoughts of home and life to be never dwindling,
A roller coaster of feelings pouring through souls,
Like soup swirling effortlessly, contained in bowls.

The shelter they had erected was certainly not spacious,
Despite this they were extremely gracious,
The slashing of wind and sand against fabric, their tent,
The storm's fierce anger was freely spent.

The two men had moved closer as best they could,
Their backs against the coarse material, wishing it were wood,
A little space, so tiny at best,
Formed between them, their bodies at rest.

So here they lay with biscuits and water,
Nak not here, his absence a torture,
How was Nak coping with the storm outside,
Same as them, wishing it over them, to quickly ride.

It was hoped that he'd curled up beside a camel,
Protection from camel, order restored as though by court's gavel,
All they could do was pray and hope,
Like a dead man pleaded to God before being hung from rope.

So Shir sat in silence as best he could in the dark,
The constant sandstorm, its continuous howl, unrestrained bark,
His thinking of Nak, his best friend that ever stood,
Even in death he'd be there, he would.

A *jemadar* without fault, no fault could he constitute in his mind,
The best man to walk the earth, never another could you find,
Only a man lacking good character could think badly of him,
Despite his scarred mouth, despite always looking grim.

# AFGHAN

Shir was a free man and lived with a free spirit,
Followed his belief to the ends of the earth, no limit,
But Nak could be followed for longer, of this he was sure,
No one on earth could salt Shir's mind, never lure.

They would all hold tight to their belief, their religion,
Would live to see the end of storm devouring this region,
Each would ride out this storm in his own way,
Even if it lasted a week they would survive its efforts to flay.

## THE DARKNESS

Before Shir and Abdul did realise,
The day had fallen, night to polarize,
Darkness from storm and shelter about,
Hard to know time of day, no aid to give shout.

Their biscuits had gone,
Shared, one by one,
Water held precious,
Forever desirous.

Boredom a tedium,
Tiredness a medium,
Wont for a mend,
For storm to end.

Shir needed to pass urine, it was time,
Pressure built, so depart tent so sublime,
He cupped his hand against Abdul's ear,
Making his intention quite clear.

Shir then departed on hands and knees,
As though grovelling, or praying to appease,
Abdul then knocking his finger in a bad way,
The throbbing pain for some time to stay.

# AFGHAN

The laziness of doing nought,
Was straining upon all thought,
With boredom this lead to tiredness,
Having achieved nothing all day, this was madness.

Shir returned not long after, to storm did beg,
Most of the urine ending on inside of leg,
But dry in short time, no need to be concerned,
Of this entire experience he would grow, would have learned.

Abdul was then startled, the feeling of crushing weight upon him,
A suffocation of ill-will, clutching to life so grim,
The sand upon shelter, upon his body, causing panic,
Difficult to move, difficult to breath, was he manic?

Shir then found Abdul's ear once more,
"What happened, I felt disturbance at your door,"
"I had a bad dream, was in its thrall,
Is Nak back yet? I wish to see him, is all."

And to what reason is he concerned over Nak's health,
What is it that transcends, a sprint over stealth,
Realization that he was to blame,
For causing Nak his facial grimace of shame.

"He will not move far amidst this storm of sand,
He will know what to do, not wander, or try to stand,
He will find shelter in one form or another,
Not allow this pestilence to grab him and smother."

"All we can do is be patient, sit the storm out,
Be optimistic, await for it to make route,
It cannot last for much longer, not more than an hour,
There's not enough sand on earth to continue this shower."

Abdul did shout into ear, cupping well, amidst their mess,
"What time do you think it is, what is your guess?"
"I have no idea," said Shir in reply,
"Even an educated guess I could not rely."

Shir said: "I think we should rest some more,
Ready our energy for what will be in store,
There will be much work after this storm has lifted,
Much devastation left in its path, much being gifted."

The two men then slept unpleasantly, off and on,
The storm ever empowering, an Italian don,
An eternity of sitting and pushing sand off body,
An eternity, soul-shattering, no melody.

Abdul had never before, in his entire life,
Never had so much time to contemplate his wife,
The friends he had treated poorly,
And those he had treated well, surely.

Question his own sanity and reason,
Whether or not to good friend he had risen,
Had been a good husband and father,
Of his home had he been master?

# AFGHAN

In reality, one was no different than another,
No tonics of life, nor character, could lather,
One may be weak, one may be strong,
There was no real right way in life, but to steer from wrong.

He would, from this day forward,
Treat each and everyone the same, self reward,
Many thoughts to himself revealed,
No way other than for actions to be appealed.

Shir too thought hard on his life,
Of all he had caused, of all the strife,
The way his life had unfolded to lead to this day,
Of mother and father, dead, in Afghanistan did lay.

Had he done the right thing in his fight against the British,
His actions as spy, forever on tenterhooks, skittish,
The long day before Shir now paved his train of thought,
A promise to never kill again, but happiness with Arika sought.

And the contemplations of life continued for them both,
In the end finding happiness within, nothing to loath,
Just promises to self that they hoped they could keep,
But for the moment all they could do was try and sleep.

## AFTERMATH AND HERDING

It was quite some time later, a marathon,
When Abdul awoke, not sure, exactly, how long,
Long enough it seemed for him to get enough sleep,
Before the wind appeared to die down, enough to take a peep.

And so he rolled over their upon the ground,
Corner of shelter lifted, once found,
Exposing a desert world for he to see,
It looked as though the storm was clearing: could it be?

And so for no reason at all of which he could account,
A panic fell over him, nervousness to start, before it did mount,
And then he closed his eyes to what he could see,
Opened them once more, to what was to be.

The tail of the storm was just passing overhead,
The sky bright and open behind it, hot day to dread,
He shook Shir awoke in order to be at the ready,
After they pray, breakfast and gather herd, upon feet unsteady.

For as he stood he almost fell over,
Bloods circulatory and its hidden power,
His feet seemed weak but confidence quick to gather,
Already his skin commencing to lather.

# AFGHAN

Neither man spoke for a minute or two,
Evaluating around them and searching for clue,
For the whereabouts of Nak and where he hid,
And call his name, Shir repeatedly did.

And from behind some shrub, mulga to adore,
A vision of pleasure fell upon them, they saw,
Nak came wandering in from fairly close by,
Feeling better than he looked he could not deny.

They all gathered and sat at what would have been their fire,
Each looking around and seeing a scene rather dire,
Equipment was strewn all over the desert floor,
And more than half the camels not at their shore.

The storm was well and truly gone, had made its pass,
Their situation quickly calculated, Nak took class,
"We have about three hours before the day does conclude,
We have to consider prayer later, camels prelude."

"We must gather the camels, herd them together,
Ensure the calf is provided Slate and with tether,
Collect the stores from about, place them beside...
Place them beside their camel, for tomorrow we ride."

"Good time we need to make on the morrow,
Good sleep and courage tonight you must borrow,
We need to make up the time lost to date,
We have to make haste, apply good speed, never be late."

Everything, all around, seemed to be covered in sand,
If it had been snow, beautiful to look at, very grand,
But this was the desert, being hot and dusty as hell,
The difference now? Camels far, far off, they could hear their bell.

"We have not a minute to lose,
We all must get the camels, follow sight and nose,
Listen hard, listen well, get the camels via best way you know,
But have yourselves a drink of water before you go."

Shir was the first upon his feet,
Three hours of daylight and night once more to greet,
With abruptness he turned to look for the camels to be netted,
Jolted by the devastation, but it had been expected.

Wool and pack saddles were strung all about,
Two thirds of the camel missing, but they were stout,
Slate and her calf were seen straight away,
The calf, to nature and impulse, did not far, from mother stray.

Sand clung to stores like glue, ridges tall,
Concave buttresses of loose sand ready to fall,
Several camels now let out lofty bellows,
Moans and groans, unabashed fellows.

A few pack saddles had been moved twenty feet or more,
Several bales of wool loose, straps shredded, tore,
But for the most it appeared not to be too bad,
But at first glance you'd think the world gone mad.

# AFGHAN

Nak considered Alfred and his wife,
They would have experienced the storm in all its rife,
They could not blame Nak if a few pounds of produce were lost,
Unfair to make the cameleers pay for the storm and its cost.

Meanwhile Shir tried with his entire might,
Listen for the bells of the camels and put things right,
And for the remainder of the day it did take,
But for good prayer and meal they did eventually make.

Nak said: "We are missing eight camels more,
But we have managed to gather all of their store,
Tomorrow we shall search here about,
And if worse comes to worst, continue our journey without.

Abdul stood up then and stepped towards Chocolate,
Removed his bell from neck before it grew too late,
Shir asked: "What are you doing, Abdul, with that?"
"Use the sound of this familiar bell, sound them out like rat."

Shir said: "Like rat. What do you mean?"
"It's called a fable, of a man, a town he did clean,
By employing music he drew all the rats from town,
Amongst the colonists the fable is renown."

Nak smiled, he knew: "I understand… yes, the bell,
This is a good plan, you are thinking well."
Nak explained briefly for Shir, unclear,
"Sound the familiar bell, the camels will come here."

Shir thought and spoke: "This is good; Abdul, a genius,
The camels will desire company, loneliness so tedious."
Abdul stepped off: "Even if it takes me all night,
All camels will be here by first light."

Nak said: "Try for two hours, no more,
Then return here, I do implore,
We shall take turns until they are found,
Bring them back here, to camping ground."

Abdul nodded his head in receipt,
Stepped off, his work to meet,
"I'll sleep," said Nak, "and then I shall take turn,
From this bad experience we all can learn."

"Oh, and Abdul," said Shir most clear,
"I shall stay by fire, most dear,
And if camels should return here by own faculty,
I shall ring a bell thrice for you, of the reality."

And so Nak went to sleep, Shir looked up to heaven,
Looking up and contemplating, life seemingly leaven,
Calamity just suffered, but here he was, alive,
Risen from the depths of despair, had not taken a dive.

The stars were out in all their glory,
Each and every one having its own story,
The moon was also, later, to offer its help,
To help light the night as the bell did yelp.

# AFGHAN

Nak was fast asleep, having suffered the most,
During the storm his soul and body almost the ghost,
He was the most worn out by the ordeal,
But now he was at rest having eaten a good meal.

Abdul could be heard from time to time,
Ringing the bell, as though in rhyme,
Three dings at a try and listening for bellow,
Though they may not holler, being rather mellow.

But by first light the next day,
Nak realised he'd not been woken, all was gay,
Abdul had found the missing camels that night,
Though four hours out he still awoke fresh and bright.

.

## CONTEMPLATIONS

Abdul did exit the tent to find the sun on its approach,
They had all slept in late, to which they did not broach,
Their morning routine commenced as per any other,
Consuming breakfast and mug of tea like lover.

Nak asked Abdul: "How is your arm this morning?"
Abdul moved it around in display, without moaning,
"It's getting much better. No red blotches on skin glowing,
Good circulation, the blood flowing."

"Probably true," said Nak, "but please don't overdo your effort,
Much of the loading of wool can me and Shir meet in comfort."
Said Abdul in response: "But the wool must get back to Marree,
Urgency there is, our reputation is sacred, we all agree."

"We're late as it is," reflected Nak. "like I said,
Contemplating further I think our situation can easily be read,
We've lost very little wool and only a few hours time,
We'll be okay with this, nothing but a little salt from lime."

Breathe sweat and tear,
Do loathers tone fear,
It matters not a little grain,
From work we do not refrain.

# AFGHAN

Hard work is not tame,
And we are not lame,
So work shall be done,
Our oath will be won.

Abdul did ask: "Will future contract be burnt like toast?"
Nak replied: "I do not wish to always boast,
But we are favoured above the oxen and horse,
Our camels are the best, always staying the course."

"I do not see how we can lose future work,
With so many jobs in shadows do lurk,
We will always come out on top,
We will win the day, we will never flop."

Abdul felt much assured by each spoken word,
Great security as though from shield and sword,
All camels had been found but some under the weather,
Hard to fathom how none had gone hell for leather.

Though not injured and just nourishment they did need,
Some redistribution was conducted, all had agreed,
Though with a working string as good as this,
It was hard to consider what further could go amiss.

They hadn't been on the road more than an hour,
When they came upon a sorrowful sight, just another to empower,
Empower and enforce great empathy within,
A small Aboriginal group on the move, product of the storm's sin.

The Aboriginal way of life seemed to be in turmoil,
The white man, of the land seeming to spoil,
Expanding into the desert regions of this country,
Taking its toll on all that once was poetry.

The way of the road for Aboriginal life,
Changed forever, for many one to strife,
But some Aboriginal people themselves also stood in their way,
Shunning any improvement, little to be gained in life everyday.

Chinese, Italians, Japanese, in this desert, this cataclysm,
Appeared to cater well for themselves amidst racism,
Improvements were coming at an extremely fast rate,
Leaps and bounds, straight from the starting gate.

Abdul had heard, though unsure on the truth,
And for this he was still rather aloof,
Alcohol with Aborigines was like stripping hair from leather,
Was their Achilles heel, their mother, their tether.

How pitiful to say or to think,
What a mess, what a stink,
To be suffocated from the land,
To castrate due to liquor, liquor mostly banned.

Aborigines absorbed with claiming rights, to make a stand,
When their dreaming proved that man did not own the land,
The land owned the people, upon which they existed,
But claiming land rights they still persisted.

# AFGHAN

Five men, four women, and six children,
Each something to portage, looking lowly as though stricken,
Vessels for carriage of water, or implement for the digging of root,
Bags or bed rolls, other utensils, a spear or two, nothing to shoot.

Several swags came into view,
Nothing special, nothing new,
Rolled within were a few condiments, dried bread, tea in a tin,
Cooked kangaroo, or wallaby, anything to feed the thin.

The camel string continued past them, going the other way,
No need to stop, no need to delay or stay,
The women were quick to ask for food as though they had none,
"*No,*" said Nak as he passed. "*No food; is all gone.*"

The sad faces of the children did hit the most,
Hitting like hammer upon head of post,
Their hands too, held out, deplorable, seemingly brittle,
Scarred from falling into campfires when little.

Shir did as Nak and ignored the pleas,
Their shallow faces, thin arms, boney knees,
But Abdul did different, being last in the line,
Reached his hand into pocket, for something on which to dine.

Giving one some jerked meat,
It was taken in silence, a silent treat,
If the other of the group had seen this, against his wish,
They would have stormed him, with open hand, with empty dish.

Nak gave Abdul a sturdy look,
A look that Abdul saw, Nak's finger then shook,
Nothing further needed to be said,
Of this lesson Abdul immediately read.

Nak had served as cameleer the longer,
Was *jemadar* and was the stronger,
Abdul had been forgetful of this lesson from the week before,
But would not allow this to happen again, it would occur no more.

By late afternoon all misery was now past,
Time for ritual, setting of camp, take advantage of all as it last,
To consider another storm approaching anytime soon,
Was far from mind, not considered, you would need to be a loon.

The episode with the bacon at homestead was recalled,
A lesson learnt here, could have seen negotiations stalled,
The differences between Christian and Muslim were not few,
Were clear to them all, it was so easy to separate the two.

Of Brother Johann Ernst Jakob and his missionary way,
No easy path for him did lay, but never did he stray,
But no sorrow could be felt for him in general,
No more than the Aborigines, their dreaming essential.

The work was hard and sometimes intolerable,
Abdul and the scorpion bite, the pain insurmountable,
Feelings of incompetence, of missed family, nothing tougher,
The responsibility each of the three held for the other.

# AFGHAN

Abdul had his family in Afghanistan,
Nak loved Saki, a love which was ban,
Shir had Arika , awarding him a grin,
They each held something close within.

They had taken all that nature threw,
But they would pull through, this they all knew,
No sandstorm or bacon could stand in their way,
Not with each of them having their say.

They were obliged to continue as best they could,
To even better the relationship with colonists as it stood,
Combined they had the reputation of good quality and spirit,
A good understanding of life in Marree as was knit.

Of Marree, other towns and settlements were similar,
Much hope they had as a business built upon strong pillar,
Like a well-built damn able to handle insurmountable weight,
Their characters would not breach, never too narrow but straight.

To do or to die was a figurative,
Nak never liked to delve into the negative,
Shir was seemingly, always so confident and sure,
Abdul hard-working, though occasionally easy to lure.

A team is a team for a contribution of differences,
Together as one as assorted meat grinds and minces,
So it was that these three men, each carved from granite,
Gave their camel string great strength, each to each a magnet.

By the time they had reached near Mulka, a confidence bolster,
They were back on schedule, not a day missed, as per roster,
Many extra miles being covered each day,
To make up everything due to the storm, their delay.

## FIVE YOUNG MEN

The three cameleers trod ever onward,
Proud of their accomplishments, it's own reward,
Misfortune and disappointment encountered along the way,
Pick themselves up they have done, from the fray.

But something more sinister was now near,
Something to impede, something to make clear,
That cameleers were not wanted here,
From this country all Afghan should steer.

They were being watched, a far-off gaze,
Through the shimmering heat, vacuum of haze,
Five pairs of young eyes looked upon them with hate,
Like fish to a hook they had come for the bait.

They had heard that a camel string was nearby,
A reliable source of talk on which they could rely,
It was spoken of three men and camels galore,
Travelling afoot, camels stacked high with store.

The five young white men barely of age to drink,
Not enough maturity to stoke fire but old enough to think,
Residents of Mulka and all that was close at hand,
This was their country and by it they would stand.

Some of their fathers had lost jobs to these few,
So their fathers had told them, so this is what they knew,
The soil beneath their feet was their honour and religion,
They would not allow these ethnics to take from the region.

This country did lack water during the summer,
It was hot as hell, drive you mad, make you stammer,
But love it they did, for it was all that they had,
Each and every thought they had was not good, was bad.

The five young men tied up their individual horse,
In the low ground of dry creek bed, a cracking course,
The area around was sparse and slightly undulating,
Scorched earth, weather dry, nothing of interest worth relating.

Snake, Horse, Bullock, Fly, Scotty: on society a stain,
Small jokes to fathers, to women folk and mothers a pain,
Christian names amongst them would never be employed,
Scotty was for Scott; easy to pressure, easily annoyed.

Snake: for he was thin and rather lean,
Bullock: he was large and rather mean,
Horse: some say gifted by nature,
Fly: for his tiny stature.

Scotty pulled a can from his saddle bag,
Held it up for his friend Fly to see, to brag,
A label wrapped around a can of bully beef,
Meat in which you could sink your teeth.

# AFGHAN

An invention of a man from the Booyoolee Station,
Adopted into the Australian psyche and this nation,
Chunks of beef drowned in gravy, pleasant smell to snout,
Now a staple that could not be lived without.

Scotty asked: "What do you say to some bully, Fly?"
Horse scolded: "Shut your mouth! If you can try,"
"Calm down, Horse," said Bullock, rather monotone, not shy,
Pushing from lip of creek, good visual it would not deny.

Continued Bullock: "They're still a ways off yet."
"I'm gonna clobber me one, damn good," said Fly in threat,
"You and what army?" said Snake, palm to cheek, stroking,
Punching Fly in shoulder, smile on face, joking.

Fly looked around, disgruntled by activity, a little perplexed,
Eager to get going, eager for what was to occur next,
To fulfil their act of revenge upon the men as they should,
By heinously striking their camels as they said they would.

"Shut up, Snake," defended Scotty, "leave him alone."
"You don't have to defend me," said Fly, feeling as thou grown,
Puffing out his chest he said: "I might be the youngest,
But I can lick those men, even their toughest."

"You won't need to," said Bullock, the eldest,
"I got me-self something hidden away, within my nest"
He then twisted and turned, drew out a rifle from hiding,
From deep within bed-roll, still upon horse, striding.

"Where the hell you get that?" asked Horse, "It's the best."
"It's me dad's rifle," replied Bullock, "Stolen from his chest."
"You're not gonna use it, are ya?" asked Horse,
"Why the hell wouldn't I?" said Bullock, "Of course, of course."

"What the hell do ya think I bought it for?
It's not for show, or to scare, but to score,
Score victory by killing their camels,
Tired I am, of seeing them on their travels."

"Scare them," protested Fly. "No; shoot the bastards!
They are nothing but stinking blacks, retards,
Those men should be killed, one and all, not just the camel,
No; hey; kill the lot, be judge and jury, heavy handed with gavel."

"No, no, no," interrupted Scotty, "that's the last straw,
We don't need any trouble with the law."
"What law?" said Snake, he too took a rifle from bed-roll,
"What the hell!" stumbled Scotty, the new reveal taking its toll.

Said Snake: "If you don't want in then go home now,
But I'm staying and will not, to these bastards bow."
"They're just men," said Horse. "Scotty's right,
The law'll get us all, so let's just give them a fright."

Said Bullock. "The closest police you will never see,
With this killing, this action, we must agree,
We're not gonna get caught, unless one of you does tell,
Unless in your weak head, consciousness sounds like a bell."

"Don't look at me, Bullock," pleaded Scotty, wishing to quit,
"I do what you think best, but I don't like it, not one bit."
"It's what they deserve," said Fly,
"Catch them, bind them, feed them pig shit from sty."

Said Scotty in appraisal: "Huh… shut up, give it a rest,
You're just power-hungry, but you're not the best."
"Hey; he's with us," said Snake, "aren't ya, Fly?"
"Sure am," answered Fly as he looked at Scotty on the sly.

And then more direct from Fly: "Ah, come on, Scotty, listen.
Them fellahs aren't even Christian."
"He's right, Scotty," said Bullock. "The lines gotta be drawn,
They're not of this country, of which I was born."

"Come on, Scotty," urged Fly, "It's the right course."
Asked Scotty: "What do you think, Horse?"
"I don't know," something inside was saying 'this is wrong'.
"Ah, come on," said Bullock. "We're in this together, five strong."

"I don't think we should," said Horse. "It aint right."
Said Snake: "If you're not with us, you and ya horse, take flight."
Horse looked around, "I'll go," prepared to move with his horse,
With the killing he could not really endorse.

"You'll go not near," insisted Bullock, "away from them you steer,
I don't want them stinking camel herders to know we're here."
"I got ya, Bullock. You don't need to tell me anything, mate,
You should change your mind, Scotty, before it's too late."

"Shut ya mouth, Horse!" said Snake as he spat,
With that said Horse turned away, "You brat."
And then to Scotty, "You know ya don't have to stay."
He stroked his horse's head before heading away.

"You're either in or out," said Bullock. "What's it going to be?"
He was going to stand his conviction, his ground, not flee,
He was tired of the cameleers, had used up all of his patience,
"I'm in," said Scotty after a little silence.

"That's great, Scotty," said Fly with a smile, "fantastic,"
Scotty simply smirked, then frowned, features elastic,
The remaining four then sought some good ground,
A position from which they had good visual all round.

What was about to unfold was the culminating, the pinnacle,
To come would break the camel's back, a cutting of iron shackle,
Bullock had failed to realise the door to Australia had opened,
Lost focus on all, peripheral blunted, not sharpened.

Many more Afghan handlers would storm this country,
A great awakening, the telegraph line but pittance, paltry,
Many advantages could be reaped after sewn,
And even in early years Australia had vastly grown.

But regardless of Bullocks knowledge on any current event,
It was near impossible to change him, no one could prevent,
Prevent what was about to unfold,
For the story which is about to be told.

# AFGHAN

But there was something else that infuriated this boy,
More than words could express, concealed as though of troy,
A story having been passed onto him,
From father to son, every word, not a single letter to trim.

Bullock told Scotty, as he stood there, the story,
A story of filth where there was found no glory,
This Afghan that they saw before them, this minute, right now,
Purposely bypassing Mulka, was a villain, tooth and nail.

They looked upon this *jemadar*, through branches and spinifex,
Lean of body, not a muscle to flex,
He was surely the one; he looked the same,
According to Bullock he was fair game.

That grin, the way his mouth presented itself,
steadfast in a grimace one would wish put to shelf,
It was said that he and several others, along this track,
Did stop near a water hole, for a wash and a snack.

But that wasn't the crime in itself, oh no, out of the question,
The crime was in ritual of prayer, their required ablution,
It was said that he removed his socks and shoes,
Washed his feet in the drinking water to wash away his woes.

"That's one of me many stories I know," said Bullock of the rot,
"It has to be stopped. I can't take no more, cannot."
Scotty looked at his friend, searching for sense, trying to lure,
"Do ya think he deserves to die?" asked Scotty, absurdly unsure.

"I do; for all he's taken from me father, for all he's done,
For all his grievances against us, for the employment won."
Snake appeared then, "Come on; you ready or what?
Get back here, spread out proper, not just stand there or squat."

The four congregated in the low ground behind some bush,
Prepared themselves as best they could, remaining hush,
Snake and Bullock taking position so as to be closest to the string,
When it passed them by they would commit an audacious sin.

## NOW FOUR YOUNG MEN

Four men, as seen through their own eyes strong,
Four boys as seen through those to whom they do wrong,
They had settled into wait and watched the caravan,
Three cameleers drawing ever closer, ready to reveal their plan.

Bullock thought little of a cameleers' life,
Heathen persons, life unforgivingly rife,
He failed to even briefly consider the work that they did,
The time they sacrificed to bring a little luxury as bid.

It was all for nothing as far as he was concerned,
Ideas quickly syphoned, intellect burnt or spurned,
He was to put to waste this unwelcome string from upon his stage,
His eyes fell to the barrel of his rifle, bullet resting, coming of age.

He'd never killed a man before,
But the hatred within him he did not deplore,
Hatred was self-motivating, the strongest urge,
Ready he was to shoot, to kill, to purge.

Snake was of dissimilar view,
Of life and death he still had no clue,
Only thought on how bad these cameleers actually were,
Ready to follow Bullock, ready to attend pot, to stir.

Snake knew of their callous ways,
Denying his father wages, removing stability, his stays,
Removed was his family's ability to put food on table,
Unable to comfortably stack merchandise to roof of stable.

For Snake the killing would come easily enough,
Never considered the consequences, whether easy or rough,
Only wishing the cameleers were on camel's back,
Further for them to fall when shot, upon ground to stack.

Questions rose within Scotty, a heavy burden, not trifle,
He wondered on the blood and guts, on the effects of a rifle,
He'd seen rabbits and dingoes killed sure enough,
Did a Afghan bleed the same as a rabbit, or was flesh tough.

Did a man squirm upon the ground in the same dying fashion,
Did he yelp like a wounded dog, was this his body's reaction?
But last of all he considered what they were about to do,
No rifle he had, and so he Picked up two large rocks in lieu.

Fly had a smile upon his face as he did watch,
The approaching string, camel kills to notch,
When he looked over and towards Bullock, the menacing look,
To his very core, he was shook.

The cameleers had no names to the young men,
But features enough to distinguish their 'humanity' from 'them',
Was it fair, was it honest, was it just,
To decide these men's fate, the young men's hatred, their lust?

# AFGHAN

Nak was at the front as usual, leading Chocolate ever so close,
To the torment that was about to befall them, about to disclose,
Shir to the centre and Abdul to the rear,
All now closer to trouble, so very near,

Nak was thinking of the love he held for Saki so bold,
He and her seemingly bound, moulded from same mould,
Shir considered his wife, for he missed her dearly,
An Aboriginal woman, different than the rest, immensely.

Shir looked upon his life with wife, they were lovers,
There was simply no way that you could compare her to others,
Those that were seen upon the desert were scroungers,
Despising life in desert to become reliant on pity, loungers.

As for Abdul, he was by far different than the other two men,
Nothing meant more to him then wife and children,
For him there was no other place on earth,
No other soil which smelled so good, devoid of turf.

## THE AMBUSH

Nak frowned, confused by the behaviour,
Chocolate becoming unsettled, acting out of flavour,
Upon the highest portion of high ground to their left,
A small lip of extended ground and a cleft.

Nak thought that a snake might suddenly appear,
His eyes scoured the area for something near,
Looking rather intently for any sign of reptilian life,
Least expecting to find the most heinous of strife.

"What is it?" asked Shir, anxiety peeking all the more,
"I'm not sure," replied Nak, eyes taking a tour,
"Chocolate senses something... I don't know... his despair."
Suddenly an unmistakable sound of a rifle shot pierced the air.

"My god!" yelled Abdul as he took to the ground,
Forgetting his finger, security to be found,
He fell with all his weight upon his hand, giving a shout,
Releasing his hold on the camel, tossing his head about.

Nak too, was quick to find comfort in security, comfort binding,
The second shot rang and he had his own rifle pulled from hiding,
"Shir," yelled Nak, seeing then a body laying flat on the ground,
"Shir; are you okay?" a question, no answer, more than profound.

# AFGHAN

There was no answer and so Abdul chanced a look,
Saw the prostrate form of his friend dead, to his core it shook,
The four Australian boys then broke from cover,
Raced down towards the three cameleers, it soon to be over.

Bullock took a brief look towards Snake with hate,
Snake having fired a little slow for his liking, too late,
But snake had killed, had made up for his poor showing,
And now the first to reach the string, knife pulled, blade glowing.

Snake's eye fell upon Shir's lifeless form as he lashed,
With knife in hand cutting the strings, Afghan lives trashed,
Camels reacted accordingly and nose pegs broke here and there,
Several camels running off still loaded, unable to care.

The kitchen camel simply pulled away,
Not for a second more would he stay,
All along the line camels reared their heads,
Breaking all connection, free of all threads.

Blood was oozing from Shir's back,
Snake callously thought, no blood did he lack,
Lying there flat, dead as an autumn leaf,
No Arika here to care, no Arika here to grief.

Abdul quickly stood as Scotty and Fly swooped past,
Slashing at all manner of string and throng to the last,
Camels buck and pull, race away, no restriction, no trouble,
No hindrance at all, no short hobble.

All of a sudden, the man named Snake,
Pulled himself up, gave himself a shake,
With clarity not to be steeped, and no delusion,
He snappily realized something amidst the confusion.

He had killed a man, dead as a doornail,
Life gone in a snuff, as easy as stepping on snail,
A great wave of guilt,
From all pores it spilt.

A great surge of sorrow leapt from him,
Had cut him short of morality, more than grim,
Why was it so important to have killed this cameleer,
Because he was from Afghanistan? He could have been a peer.

So hard it was to consider enemy and ally,
Where was the truth, was it standing nearby,
This man was living flesh, spoke, ate, and walked,
Now he was condemned to hell, Snakes belief, balked.

Like smoke on the air, no tobacco to inhale,
Putrid air and life, life which now felt stale,
And whilst he stood their considering this life poorly,
His comrades continued to cause all manner of strife most surely.

Fly grabbed hold of a camel, quick as a flash,
It then bit his hand, a nasty gash,
Fly pulled the hand back from the pain and fright,
Before thrusting his knife into camels throat: good night.

# AFGHAN

Abdul was able to hit hard Fly in the side of the leg,
Whom fell upon the ground, brief cry of pain to beg,
Abdul rallied his strength, pulled himself upon the coward,
Commenced lashing out with closed fists, the strings steward.

Steward for he cared for the kitchen camel,
Cared for the camel during their trek as they travel,
Scotty then came in from behind, unknown,
Began with his own bout of fists, rapidly thrown.

With the pain of his amputated finger recalled and then forgotten,
Abdul now had to contend with a flurry of new pain most rotten,
Blind punches to the kidney, it was thereabout,
The pain, gaping mouth, no air, no audible shout.

Fly was upon his feet in seconds and prepared to run,
Scotty close on his heels, away from danger, this was no fun,
Bullock, meanwhile, having forgotten to reload his rifle,
Now lashed out with butt of weapon against Nak's jaw to stifle.

An audible crack could be heard,
It was as though the world had been stirred,
Nak grasp his own rifle heartedly as he fell,
Bullock took no time, no thought, no spell.

He continued with his merciless killing spree,
Quickly reloading weapon, bringing a camel to its knee,
By this time Nak had gathered his senses, powered from within,
Pulled his rifle up near slightly cracked jaw, his head in a spin.

Nak took a sight picture, time having slowed down,
Slight contortion to mouth, a scowl, and then a frown,
But he couldn't do it, not even now,
Tired of death, from death he took a bow.

But no, this was wrong, bright in head were the lights,
Fly suddenly appeared within his sights,
Nak fired a single shot whereby Fly fell down dead,
Nak was not happy, not sad, no identity on face could be read.

"NO!" yelled Scotty who went to his aid amidst the fray,
Tripped over then by Abdul from where he lay,
His face came down hard upon the ground in a streak,
His nose breaking, now flat against cheek.

Snake suddenly shook the reality of the dead man from mind,
The fourth rifle shot fired shook him awake, reality he did find,
He saw his friend, Fly, fall hard upon the ground and knew,
Right there, Fly was dead, sorrow now exponentially grew.

## THE SINGLE RETURNS

Horse heard the first of the rifle shots in the distance,
The attack had commenced, the boys and their deliverance,
He should have done more in preventing this from occurring,
Instead of within, thinking of self, contemplating, purring.

On hearing the second shot, he pulled upon the reigns of his horse,
Steered it away and to a halt from its present course,
He commenced contemplation, his thoughts not easily read,
The third shot then sang out and Horse turned his head.

He commenced riding towards his friends, slow moving,
They having been left to their own vices, their evil doing,
Suddenly overcome with different emotions,
Many scenarios forming in his head, many notions.

The fighting within himself was little more than a question,
Good over bad, bad over good: not yet an answer to equation,
Bullock wanted, by the sounds of things, to hinder, to bend,
To scatter their camels, ruin their truck, to entirely amend.

The death of the cameleers was simply a bonus,
Bullock wished to feed his desire, independent, autonomous,
Horse, not sure why he was returning; Conviction? Mind strong?
A feeling within, as though something had gone wrong.

For at the same time of his thinking the fourth shot had sounded,
Different than the others, more rounded,
For he knew each calibre held a different tone,
And the sound he had heard struck him to the bone.

This fourth shot fired made all the difference,
By its sound he could see it, make out its appearance,
He was now trotting at a reasonably good speed,
Suiting his desire, fitting his need.

He'd now reached the point just half way between,
Where Bullock had chosen, of heathen to clean,
He pulled at his horse and listened well,
Something not far off, he could tell.

"Bullock," said Horse, "is that you?",
Why did he ask that, he had no real clue,
Still, Bullock lifted his head from behind some brush,
No longer so alive, no longer so lush.

He was followed by Snake whom held his head low,
Gone from him too was the usual glow,
Horse dismounted and walked over to where they were crouched,
Saw them both filled with grief, their look, the way they slouched.

Horse knelt down beside the two,
"Where's Fly and Scotty?" he asked, but he knew,
The silence that followed was clear, but clarity askew,
"Were they killed?" asked Horse, and his anxiety grew.

# AFGHAN

Bullock looked him in the eye, "Scotty was captured."
"And Fly?" asked Horse, wishing to be told, to be lectured,
"He's dead," said Snake flatly, no semblance of grace,
"I saw him, before I got away," now looking Horse in face.

"Where's your rifle?" asked Horse of Snake for more, even a clue,
"He left it behind," said Bullock. "Now they have two—."
Snake hit Bullock in the face, quickly set upon by Horse,
Friend hitting friend he could not truly endorse.

"That's enough; no more!" commanded Horse,
Not wishing to take this road, wishing to change course,
"I'm more worried about Fly and Scotty than quibbling,
Not your puns, blaming, scolding, wild accusations scribbling.

"It's no good," insisted Snake. "Fly is horse meat, dead,
I know, I saw it, to body a shot from Afghan rifle fed,
Now eternally put to bed,
Never to live life, never to wed."

Horse asked: "So what happened to ya rifle?"
"I guess I dropped it, amidst the scuffle."
"Dropped it!" repeated Bullock sarcastically,
"Enough," stabbed Horse. "We gotta think now, logically."

"We can't just leave Scotty there with those... men,
But it's a matter of acting now, not when."
"I don't think I can do any more," said Snake. "I feel sick inside,
This is not what I signed on for, this is not the ride."

"You should have thought about that earlier," said Horse,
"But it's too late now, so stop feeling remorse,
Instead of feeling sad and dejected,
Consider Scotty, who will not be neglected."

"I still got me rifle," said Bullock, straight to the meat of the bone,
"I don't know," said Horse. "They have two, we have one."
"We'll shoot first and ask questions later."
"That isn't funny, Bullock," spat Snake of the matter.

"No one said it was," said Bullock. "We have to go in ready,
We have no choice now but to go in fast but steady."
"You're right," said Horse. "I don't think we have a choice."
"I killed one of them," came Snake, sound from cracking voice.

Snake looked up dismayed and sad,
Feeling the horrors of his deed growing, having been so bad,
Said Bullock: "Don't feel guilty for what you done,
We still have much to do, they're the losers, they haven't won."

"He's right," agreed Horse looking into Snake's eye,
"We have to save Scotty, in the by-and-by,
And your horses, where are they?"
"Lost; our whistle amidst commotion they would not obey."

Concluded Horse: "Then we'll have to retrieve them,
For a horse thief I shall never accept, but always condemn,
Assuming, that is, the horses are with the cameleers,
...I shall rip out their brains, their minds, from between ears."

## THE AFGHANS COALESCE

Shir had been laid in a blanket once able,
Placed in the shade of a tree most suitable,
Picturesque as can be beside the dry creek bed,
Flies trying to annoy whilst with heaven his spirit was lead.

Said Nak: "The flies I hate the worse, so rude,
Poor Shir is dead and all they want is to intrude,
"Forever a pest, never at rest, in our eyes and ear,
And now, even after death, they swarm and appear.

Asked Abdul of the *jemadar*: "What do we do? Flee or stay?"
Nak looked over to where the body of Fly did lay,
Felt as though he had let the team down, a heavy disgrace,
Did nothing to prevent the onslaught from taking place.

"Allow the maggots their feast upon his sin, we must agree,"
And then he looked to the other, tied to the base of a tree,
Said Nak then to the other:. *"What name you, boy?"*
*"Why you is kill us, why you try to... destroy?"*

Scotty didn't answer at first; he had a broken nose,
Caked in blood, smelly from sweat, bruised from fight, no rose,
Truly bruised and bloody he was with two black eyes,
Looking a match, peas to a pod, for sinner a suitable guise.

Nak stood up and hurried to him; swiftly, boldly,
Before he could lash out with a kick so unkindly,
He screamed out and tried to curl into a ball,
"SCOTTY!" the kick didn't come at all.

Scotty shaking from his ordeal,
"My name is Scotty and very sick I feel."
*"You friend coward, run quick, run fast,
Much far away now, such friendship not last."*

*"You horse now mine, you nothing, you see.
I get pretty good money of horse for me."*
"I don't think he cares," pointed out Abdul of the matter,
Seemingly not caring that his friends did scatter.

Now Scotty was more concerned for his life,
In the hands of these heathen, life on edge of knife,
He knew he could walk home from where they were,
Just needed that opportunity, that chance to stir.

Abdul did ask: "What are we to do now?"
"We'll have to tell the police, Scotty's arse we'll tow,
Hand the boy into the authorities, into jail they'll throw,
Tell them the story and then they'll know."

"I don't see any other alternative, there is none to voice,
I don't exactly trust the police but we do not have a choice,
We can't let the boy go because he'll tell lies: one who deceives,
We could end up being convicted of murder, and horse thieves."

## AFGHAN

"But with the boy in custody, delivered in bonds, sing our song,
Along with the horses to hand over as proof, and proof is strong,
I think we can fairly well sell our story,
Of self-defence and the savagery most gory."

"I think we should also cover the boy's body, in order to protect,
Before the maggots eat too much, but for him I have little respect,
Leaving him to be eaten, his body already spindly,
The police nor his parents will take kindly—."

"I don't care, Abdul," interrupted Nak, "do you hear,
The people can think what they like, both far and near,
I'm sick to death of them all, I am shattered, I am busted,
Even those we offer good service, none of them can be trusted."

Abdul did ask: "When will we leave?"
"Tomorrow morning," said Nak, "but give me time to grieve,
We'll take the few camels we have remaining,
 Along with the horses, with what food we have, for sustaining."

"The horses can be used to carry the dead,
The white man's ride, now a bed,
The prisoner we'll make walk for a while, put him out of shape ,
After he's so tired he'll not want to escape."

"What about the other camels; the lost, the quick?"
"They'll have to stay lost for now, to our plan we stick,
Maybe we can come back for them, even if late,
We still have the bells from Chocolate and Slate."

"What of the wool that remains, that we have here,
Not much to speak of but our promise was clear."
"You're right," said Nak. "I'll consider it tonight."
"The others may return, they still have a rifle in order to fight."

"We have two," said Nak and then thought of the wool,
"They have no transport, to chase on foot they would be a fool,
We have three camels and four horses, with  no time to saunter,
We have lost our stores, have little food and little water."

"My Koran is gone along with our prayer mats,
We have nothing left but pesky flies and a few gnats,
But tonight we'll maintain watch, be as silent as a ghost,
We can set up a small watching post."

"We will set up a fire so it can be easily seen,
Set a trap just in case, our turn to be mean,
If they approach the fire then they must be shot,
We can't afford to be caught unaware, simply cannot."

"They have the advantage," said Abdul knowingly,
"But we have a prisoner and two rifles," added Nak surprisingly."
Abdul said: "I'm just concerned for my family, my wife,
I don't really care for my own life."

"My family back at home will never know what happened,
They will be devastated to never hear of me again, saddened."
"Your wife loves you, Abdul. That's the truth, not a lie."
"And what about you, Nak? Are you afraid to die?"

# AFGHAN

"There is life after death, dear friend of mine,
I will be 42 years old for eternity: so hard to define,
72 virgins for me, ready to tend my every need,
What more could a man ask from heaven? Nothing indeed."

And he thought then of Saki and his love,
His Snow White, his sacred dove,
"It's good for you," said Abdul, endeavouring to make a joke,
"Me 23 and you 42: bestowed upon you a toke."

Said Nak: "But that will not affect your enjoyment of a virgin."
Abdul smiled: "You're right, still it's too many for me to imagine,
I'll give you some of mine, something to remember, a wreath."
"Ha!" yelped Nak. "Any more and I'll die a second death."

A serious look now falls over Abdul, now a little blue,
"Nak… there's something I have to tell you."
"It's about the battle of Char Asiab?"
Abdul was stunned. "Ah, it is; what a guess, a good stab."

"You fought with the British and I against, against them rotten,
It doesn't matter, Abdul. It's okay; it's forgotten."
Abdul was now more serious than before: "No, something more."
"What?" asked Nak. "What else is there in the cup to pour?"

"That scar on your face; your lips, the one that does mar."
Nak gently passes his fingertips over the horrendous scar,
"It was me. I was the one that wounded you, a scar to stay."
Nak looks at Abdul closely and waved the thought away.

"No; you're mistaken," insisted Nak of the comment,
"I was in Char Asiab, my actions consecrated in cement,
I was in conflict with you, Nak. I saw you get hit,
Out from your defensive position... everything does fit."

"I saw the injury upon your face...I saw your face,
Nak... I know it was you, and I feel a tremendous disgrace."
Nak said: "It could have been any man that fired that shot,
It could have been anyone that fired.... Could it not?"

Abdul smiles lightly and holds out his hand, most sincere,
Nak hesitates and then accepts it, in Abdul's eye a little tear,
"I'm sorry, Nak... truly, for your many years of pain,
For all of these years in which I, upon your body, did stain."

They hold hands for a few seconds and then release their hold,
Nak said: "It wasn't you, Abdul. Even if it was how you just told,
I forgive you. For ever and a day, from this time forward."
"You're my friend, Nak; a true friend, life's reward."

## A FINAL STAND

Snake quickly lead the way, Bullock in wake of tide,
Horse lead his horse on foot to match their stride,
The advance was suddenly brought to a temporary close,
Snake put up a hand for halt, scratched his nose.

Asked Bullock: "What is it? What do you see up front?"
"Another camel," and looking to Bullock did grin and grunt,
Bullock lifted rifle into shoulder, looked down the sight,
Seeing the animal he then held his rifle tight.

Horse approached from behind and slammed his palm down,
Expression bane with voice tampered, a growl and a frown,
"Don't be foolish; idiot. Don't act foolishly, filled with remorse."
"Damn; that hurt," said Bullock as he looked at Horse.

"Think before you act,
Get hold of the fact,
We are one rifle, they are men, all three,
They have the advantage... agree!"

Bullock said: "I do agree with some,
But we have advantage of surprise, don't be dumb,
But, yes, I agree we should approach in silence,
I just feel like shooting camels, having been given a new license."

"I got a better idea," said Snake and stepped off,
"What are you doing?" asked Horse, "Stop acting the toff."
"Do ya want these camels to fester the land?" Snake did ask,
"Walking around, drinking at ease, eating for free, free to bask?"

Snake approached the camel for his statement they did accept,
The sun slowly disappearing below the horizon as he crept,
He crept ever closer, more slowly as he closed the gap,
Getting closer to camel, bringing camel to lap.

The nerves of the camel had simmered,
Easy it was to approach untethered,
He was not wild but tame,
Had a slight limp and so was lame.

Snake moved his hands to axe handle and took a good grip,
Not wishing to allow good aim to slip,
Once satisfied and close enough he swung hard and low,
The camel's leg broke as too did his bellowing grow.

He quickly finished the job off in the best way he knew,
Hitting hard upon head the skull splitting in two,
Streams of red came out as a flood,
Axe now covered in membranes and blood.

Bullock approached Snake and the dead mass upon the ground,
The killing he too enjoyed, surprised happiness could be found,
"Come on, Snake, that's enough," he too gratified a tonne,
"It's dead now; give it a rest will ya? Let's get on, you've won."

# AFGHAN

Snake stopped pounding down upon the carcass, did display vain,
"I'm sick of these bloody animals, this desert they stain,
Good for nothing is what they are, enough I have had,
Taking what work is available away from me and my dad."

"It's not just you," said Horse as he drew alongside,
"We all suffer, and these heathens, our rules they don't abide."
"And now it's time they suffered," said Snake,
"We'll wait till it gets fully dark, comb this land with rake."

Snake continued: "Mmmm…. They'll need a fire for that matter,
I'm sure they will; and then their lives we can shatter."
Said Horse: "You're right, and help Scotty, great idea I think.."
Snake said: "Agreed. Let's get out of here; this camel does stink."

## TWO AFGHAN MEN

The sky above was a brilliant dark blue: serine, mature,
A peaceful reminder, man a small part of a larger picture,
Abdul didn't know much about the heavens so bright,
But knew enough to find his way around at night.

He was sitting next to a large bush,
Facing the campfire as it burnt so lush,
Brightness evaporating into the cold of night,
The edge between light and dark, a sheer delight.

A few night creatures sounding now and then,
Scurrying along small crevices, folds in land, a small glen,
And coupled with the light from sky so high above,
All fitting together, serenity, peas in pod, fingers in glove.

Abdul was content to sit where he was for half the night,
To await the boys he knew would return to fight,
He had both rifles with him: he was highly strung, did not tire,
A round of ammunition up the spout of each, ready to fire.

Nak rolled over in his sleep,
From Scotty, stretched out near the tree, not a peep,
He'd had a gag placed over mouth in order to prepare,
To ready their trap, to ready their snare.

# AFGHAN

A bed roll had been placed out beside the fire,
The dead man Shir, lay here, by Nak's desire,
To trick the others into believing him alive,
Net of trap now set, some lives to take a dive.

Abdul cocked his head a little, heard a horse, far or near?
He couldn't be sure but it was audibly clear,
He strained his ears, leaning his head a little to the side,
The silhouette of a single figure coming out from hide.

Abdul looked over towards where Scotty was lying, dead asleep,
Knew immediately that he was overtired, the night now to keep,
And then another two figures appeared out of nowhere,
Light from the fire revealed the front figure in slight glare.

He wasn't carrying a rifle and so one of the others held that,
A little too close for comfort, Abdul dare not move, eyelids bat,
Abdul decided what to do, mentally tired through and through,
Had sworn to treat all the same, but this he could no longer do.

And so this was the reality of his promise to self,
Forced to put all consciousness to shelf,
For he knew there was a rifle amongst the three,
But hard it was, even amidst light of fire, to clearly see.

Abdul lifted his rifle and without a shadow of a doubt,
Squeezed the trigger of the rifle, fire from muzzle to sprout,
The loud firing of rifle enough to wake the devil,
Drawing the playing field now to level.

For the shot was a success and Snake fell down hard, rolled over,
Wounded in the stomach from which he would not recover,
A heavy gasp for air erupted from him as he commenced to die,
To soon go visit hell, and for eternity to fry.

Nak stirred silently awake,
All reality did receive a good shake,
For Bullock two targets to shoot, one with weapon, the threat,
Time for him to avenge, time for body count to be net.

Having not taken good aim as Abdul had endeavoured to do,
Bullock did miss, firing wide, making a blue,
And so Bullock did panic, he did blunder,
Haphazardly firing his rifle and hitting Abdul in the shoulder.

Abdul did not feel the pain just then from the hit,
Adrenaline coursing through body, hole in flesh ready to knit,
Abdul quickly had the second rifle in is hand,
With swift ease and of great steadiness of skill he did demand.

He pulled the trigger this time, anxious, shooting instinctively,
It hitting Bullock square in the head, killing him instantly,
Bullock's body fell like a sack of spuds upon the desert canopy,
Abdul and Nak now held complete monopoly.

Horse raced over to where Bullock did so heavily fall,
His mind clear and decisive, a power to which he was in thrall,
Understood fully the predicament he and his friends had attained,
He picked the rifle up for the fight to be maintained.

# AFGHAN

Gasps of pain,
No playing lame,
Grunts of shame,
Everyone to blame.

Nak was now upon his feet and raced towards Horse,
Snake on brink of death kicked out with much pain of course,
The sheer effort, all he had, enough to tax him hard,
But of all his commitment he would not give a yard.

The bleeding of Snake was largely internal,
Like a volcano bursting its banks, ever infernal,
Larva now spouting from the top,
Great pressure within not willing to stop.

Snake gasped for air then, drawing on every effort of breath,
But no more breath came, all was left was death,
Snake died, last fragment of thought, his family at home, he alone,
Here he was, seemingly dying like a dog without bone.

Nak fell hard upon the ground having been tripped,
A blade of spinifex forced into his eye, all sanity now nipped,
The shock of the fall and the pain from protrusion,
There was nothing to paint of this, but pain, and no illusion.

Horse had soon found some ammunition and loaded this into slot,
He brought the weapon into his shoulder and took a shot,
At near point-blank range Nak's body mass hit… life spent,
Nak's stirring fell silent…………………...

Abdul saw all of this, everything more,
Nak's life spent, now at heaven's door,
And who now was alive, who was dead,
What was left, what can be said.

It was now that the pain in his arm commenced to build,
Gone was the adrenaline, gone was his shield,
He fumbled around for what he had placed beside his knee,
Found the ammunition for rifle and reloaded it with little glee.

He brought the weapon up into his shoulder as best he could,
The weapon, the pain, he then stalled as he felt he would,
Horse threw his rifle to the ground, an audible thudding sound,
He saw Scotty motionless, there bound upon the ground.

Horse's weaknesses was the fact that he'd just shot a man,
Going to hell was never his plan,
Horse was in a flurry, unsure what he should do,
Kneeling beside Scotty, knife in his hand, his life was through.

Abdul couldn't believe the stupidity, this methodical thinking,
How he'd simply raced up to his friend, amongst all this killing,
Maybe these whites were not much different than he,
Maybe they were the same, more to meet the eye, more to see.

Abdul would not have shot at a defenceless cameleer,
As they made their way from town to town amidst sneer,
Endeavouring to earn a little money for bread,
And characteristically out of nowhere, Abdul shot Scotty dead.

# AFGHAN

He had squeezed the trigger, given hope to Horse,
Shot Scotty, the bound, the end of remorse,
To let Horse live, seemingly the most healthy,
To live and grow of knowledge wealthy.

Horse heard the shot fired, it was dire,
Saw blood erupt from Scotty by the light of the fire,
Horse felt he understood then the meaning of life,
The meaning was death, whether from old age, rifle or knife.

Nak had instinctively reloaded his rifle, senselessly relating,
Despite considering his life at an end, hangman's rope waiting,
Horse felt he was up against better men, death a formality,
Didn't wish to be a statistic, landing back to reality.

*"You go,"* shouted Abdul. *"You go long way, no come back,*
*You got horse, you take and go home. No more attack,*
*Me forget quick. Me not care. You live, me live; we both live,*
*You know what meaning is; you understand what it is I give?"*

"Yes," replied Horse. "I know what you mean: it's the end."
Horse looked down into the closed eyes of his friend,
Of the five he was the only one left living,
"You've killed four of my friends. That's hard giving."

Lectured Abdul: *"Alive is good, dead is bad,*
*You go and me go. We both go, both sad."*
"Yes," said Horse as he stood, sheathing his knife, there to stay,
"We both go." Horse turned and commenced to move away.

He stumbled to a stop, had something to say,
"Thank you," he said and continued on his way,
"*Okay,*" said Abdul. "*You do thing, one more for me,
You make horse speak, me know you gone, we no longer see.*"

"Yes; yes, okay," said Horse, understanding all,
Abdul wished to ensure that upon him again he did not fall,
"But I'll be back tomorrow, for they I cannot neglect,
Just leave them alone and give them a little respect."

> "*Okay. I leave horses here too,
> Me with them is through,
> They not clean as camel,
> Hard to… make travel.*"

## ABDUL'S DEMISE AND RETURN TO ROOTS

Abdul was on foot now and staggering a little,
He'd patched his wound as best he could, feeling brittle,
He'd left the bodies of the whites behind,
But his friends were with him, on this long grind.

Nak and Shir were strapped to two of their camel,
The third carried a little water, nothing left on which to marvel,
The thought of riding upon the camel hadn't been considered,
Such was the decay of his normality, mentality slivered.

His thinking was askew, thoughts mostly of the past,
His first real job here was also his last,
Nak Kadir was from Kabul, aged 42 and single,
Shir Adji was from Karachi, married to Arika, was subtle.

He would remember them forever and ever, always,
No matter where, the houses, the countries, the opened doorways,
But for now he had to fend for himself and deliver his friends,
Get back to civilization, across sparseness, around unseen bends.

He looked down upon the sand, town far from drawing nigh,
Unable to see his shadow for the sun was high in the sky,
Daydreaming and staggering, he'd had no sleep the night before,
Looking up as he went: was it real or illusion, that which he saw?

And a few more seconds was all he could endure,
The calling of unconsciousness, lack of blood the lure,
When he fell it was silently and fast,
Upon this heated furnace so open and vast,

But then the jolting of the wagon woke Abdul up from the rear,
And the stirrings of a familiar voice echoed in his ear,
Said Johann: "Ah, praise the good Lord that you have risen,
You've been in and out of your daze for a day, now listen."

"How do you feel?
Hungry for food, for a meal?"
Abdul understood enough of what was said,
But still had a lot of blurriness to contend with in his head.

He rubbed at his eyes and it was suddenly clear,
Of the pain in his shoulder, death of friends, and the fear,
Said Johann: "Ah; I fixed that as best I could,
Took some mending, but flesh is not wood."

*"Where we go?"* asked Abdul for news of his predicament,
"I found you beside the track, unconscious for the moment,
I was heading north but decided to turn back to Maree,
The least I can do for a man, even one like you, hope you agree."

*"Where friend?"* Abdul's question a flurry, did smother,
"What friend? Ah; you mean the other?
I don't know. You know; I thought it was weird, a bit strange,
That they should leave you alone like that upon this desert range."

# AFGHAN

"Did one of them shoot you; were they filled with dread?"
"*No. You no see friends? They dead...*
*No, no. Not meaning. Friend is dead; you find;*
*You see them and camels?*" asked Abdul, words hard to bind.

"Are they dead? I don't know," said Johann: to him it did confuse,
"Here, have a drink," Johann handed him water, began to muse,
"No, I didn't see anyone. No camels, no friend,
Just you; and lucky I did, for you were near your end."

Abdul thought on the past, the hellish weather,
Nak and Shir were strapped, bound with leather,
The camels surelly taken off, possibly in search of water and food,
The bodies of his friends lost forever, forever to allude.

Said Johann: "We shouldn't be long into Marree,
"You'll have to report this to the police, you and me... we."
Abdul considered what was said,
This was a problem, deep issue, not easily read.

Without the bodies of Nak and Shir... evidence gone,
What was he to tell the police, his story could not be hone,
The circumstances of being shot could not be proven,
The white boy, on other hand, could bake any story in oven.

Maybe it was time to let sleeping ghosts lie,
Say nothing of what had happened, just simply deny,
He should try and return to Afghanistan whilst he had the chance,
No need to make a storm in a teacup, no need to shout and dance.

"*No,*" said Abdul, loud enough to hear,
Said Johann: "No! It's not my place to say, but Maree is near,
But I think justice should be done, nail on head, a heavy stone,
To those that left you there to die in great misery and all alone."

"*I forgive, and forget,*" but Abdul wasn't so sure that he could,
Never forget the ordeal he'd suffered, never would,
"I'll take you to the Ghantown then," Johann did offer,
"Would you like that? It would not be any bother."

Abdul smiled, looked up at Johann, looked him in the face,
"*You good friend,*" said Abdul with much sincere grace,
"*You good man this place. Me never forget.*"
And of all the week's misery he honestly had nothing to regret.

Abdul had not caused the fight with the boys,
He treated all fairly, filled lives with many joys,
Never did throw the first stone,
Had even apologized to Nak, did atone.

Johann simply smiled and turned his eyes again upon the track,
Life in Australia was too hard, to Afghanistan he would go back,
He smiled and thanked God for he had survived by a mere margin,
What would he do in heaven with seventy-two women all virgin?

www.ingramcontent.com/pod-product-compliance
Lightning Source LLC
Chambersburg PA
CBHW020144120726
47903CB00007B/2412